THE HONOURED

ARKAN DARDANUS RUNS. He runs hard, as hard as his powered plate will allow. About him are fields, where dark crops dance in the breeze. The wind is at the veteran's armoured back – the air pushed forth ahead of the cataclysm unfolding behind. It is madness. It is death.

'I am the fist,' Dardanus recites, '*clenched tight in ceramite, smashing with the force of a Legion. I am the blade, awaiting my foe's flesh, as keen as the Emperor could make me. I am the bolt, fired from afar – fleet and true, an end to all who stand before the Imperium of Man.*'

The words are not his. They belong, like many good words, to his primarch. Their purpose is to combat confusion with clarity, to banish doubt and reinforce a legionary's purpose. As Dardanus's hearts thunder in his chest, he feels Guilliman with him, urging him on.

THE HORUS HERESY®

Other Novels and *Novellas*

PROMETHEAN SUN
Nick Kyme

AURELIAN
Aaron Dembski-Bowden

BROTHERHOOD OF THE STORM
Chris Wraight

THE CRIMSON FIST
John French

PRINCE OF CROWS
Aaron Dembski-Bowden

DEATH AND DEFIANCE
Various authors

TALLARN: EXECUTIONER
John French

SCORCHED EARTH
Nick Kyme

THE PURGE
Anthony Reynolds

THE HONOURED
Rob Sanders

THE UNBURDENED
David Annandale

RAVENLORD
Gav Thorpe

Many of these titles are also available as abridged and unabridged audiobooks.
Order the full range of Horus Heresy novels and audiobooks from
blacklibrary.com

Download the full range of Horus Heresy audio dramas from
blacklibrary.com

Also available

THE HORUS HERESY®

Rob Sanders

THE
HONOURED

Betrayal at Calth

BLACK LIBRARY

For TC, Jonah and Elliot – you know why…

A BLACK LIBRARY PUBLICATION

Hardback edition published in 2015.
This edition published in Great Britain in 2015.
Black Library,
Games Workshop Ltd.,
Willow Road,
Nottingham,
NG7 2WS, UK.

10 9 8 7 6 5 4 3 2 1

Produced by the Games Workshop Design Studio.

A CIP record for this book is available from the British Library.

UK ISBN: 978 1 78496 246 3
US ISBN: 978 1 78496 247 0

See Black Library on the internet at

blacklibrary.com

Find out more about Games Workshop
and the world of Warhammer 40,000 at

games-workshop.com

Printed and bound by CPI Group (UK) Ltd, Croydon, CR0 4YY

The Horus Heresy

It is a time of legend.

The galaxy is in flames. The Emperor's glorious vision for humanity is in ruins. His favoured son, Horus, has turned from his father's light and embraced Chaos.

His armies, the mighty and redoubtable Space Marines, are locked in a brutal civil war. Once, these ultimate warriors fought side by side as brothers, protecting the galaxy and bringing mankind back into the Emperor's light.
Now they are divided.

Some remain loyal to the Emperor, whilst others have sided with the Warmaster. Pre-eminent amongst them, the leaders of their thousands-strong Legions are the primarchs. Magnificent, superhuman beings, they are the crowning achievement of the Emperor's genetic science. Thrust into battle against one another, victory is uncertain for either side.

Worlds are burning. At Isstvan V, Horus dealt a vicious blow and three loyal Legions were all but destroyed. War was begun, a conflict that will engulf all mankind in fire. Treachery and betrayal have usurped honour and nobility. Assassins lurk in every shadow. Armies are gathering.
All must choose a side or die.

Horus musters his armada, Terra itself the object of his wrath. Seated upon the Golden Throne, the Emperor waits for his wayward son to return. But his true enemy is Chaos, a primordial force that seeks to enslave mankind to its capricious whims.

The screams of the innocent, the pleas of the righteous resound to the cruel laughter of Dark Gods. Suffering and damnation await all should the Emperor fail and the war be lost.

The age of knowledge and enlightenment has ended.
The Age of Darkness has begun.

~ DRAMATIS PERSONAE ~

The XIII Legion 'Ultramarines'

ROBOUTE GUILLIMAN	Primarch, Lord of The Five Hundred Worlds of Ultramar
TAURO NICODEMUS	Tetrarch of Ultramar (Saramanth), Primarch's Champion
REMUS VENTANUS	Captain, Fourth Company
STELOC AETHON	Captain, 'The Honoured 19th' Company
IMBRIUS MEDON	[seconded to command duties]
ORESTRIAN URCUS	Sergeant, Terminator Squad Urcus
LEPIDUS	
EPHANOR	
PHALON VICTURUS	
EUROTAS	
NEREON	
DACTYS	
ANDRON PONTUS	
HESTOR	
MIDON ASTERIAX	
THASANDER	
PALAEMON	
LADON	
SCAMANDER	

SALVATAR SEPHIRUS	Sergeant, Squad Sephirus
GALEN	
SCAERON	
PTOLEMUS	
PHANTOR	
ARKAN DARDANUS	[acting sergeant, Squad Sephirus]
IOLCHUS TIBOR	
SOLARIUS	
VANTARO	
SARAMAN ALOYSIO	
HADRIAX	
LAERTUS	
EURYMACHON	
FIDUS GALTARION	Sergeant, Squad Galtarion
NYSUS	
TYNON	Sergeant, Squad Tynon
DEUCALIUS CHALCODON	
AUTOLO	[rotated to active duties]
PHERONEUS DAEDAL	[sergeant, rotated to active duties]
XANTIUS DOLOMON	[rotated to active duties]
ENDYMIAS	[rotated to active duties]
IDAS	[sergeant, rotated to active duties]
LANTOR	[sergeant, rotated to active duties]
LYCASTUS	[rotated to active duties]

DROMEDON PAX   [rotated to active duties]

PHAELON   [sergeant, rotated to active duties]

PHINEON   [sergeant, rotated to active duties]

PRONAX   [rotated to active duties]

PYRAMON   [rotated to active duties]

ULANTUS REMULO   [rotated to active duties]

RENDRUS   [sergeant, rotated to active duties]

CYDOR RHADAMANTH   [rotated to active duties]

SARPEDUS   [sergeant, rotated to active duties]

SERAPHO   [rotated to active duties]

TITHONON   [assumed command
                      of the *Aeternian*]

VALIN   [sergeant, rotated to active duties]

HYLAS PELION   Honorarius, 82nd Company

The XVII Legion 'Word Bearers'

KURTHA SEDD   Chaplain [marked for capture]

MALDREQ FAL   Sergeant

SHAN VAREK   [rank unknown]

UNGOL SHAX   Chaplain

ONE

When is a lie not merely a lie, Aethon wonders? *When do such words fail to capture the enormity of untruths so thunderous in their announcement that, like a black hole, they exert a gravity of their own, causing the light of truth to bend about them?*

Steloc Aethon, captain of the 19th Company, 'The Honoured'.

He is an Ultramarine, a son of Guilliman. He is a son of Calth.

The havoc of Lanshear roars about him. Gunfire. Murder. Desperation. Armoured Word Bearers, their suits the colour of dried blood. Ultramarines, their immaculate plate besmirched with ash and gore. Aethon hears the muted screams of the traitors along with the death cries of his own men, harsh and horrified across the vox. Punctuated by the drum of boltguns, it is a cacophonous symphony of betrayal and despair.

Are the Ultramarines not the light that bends? The Emperor's light, illuminating the far reaches of his empire, contorted about falsehoods terrible and true. Are the sons of Guilliman forever changed by the wretched unfolding of these great events? Will we stand, like shadows of our former selves, in the brilliance of reali-sation – as we stand now before the wrath of Veridia?

Within the ceramite confines of his Tactical Dreadnought armour the battle seems removed, even with death but a moment away. The treachery of men Aethon once called kin plays out before him like an impossible dream – his own actions, a whirlwind of murderous necessity, simi-larly so. The tactical display, targeting reticules and the overlapping vox-streams reporting the carnage beyond seem removed further still. Calth is a world betrayed. A planet brought to its knees. Within hours the bounteous sustenance of agricultural toil has been transformed into a nightmare of disbelief, smoke-shrouded battlefields and global slaughter.

Orders proceed, almost unconsciously, from the captain's drawn lips. The genhanced muscle of his transhuman body works the massive Terminator suit around. His gauntlets yank back on the trigger of his combi-weapon and gun his chainfist to shrieking annihilation. Aethon's mind is else-where, however. He kills without thinking. His commands are the living, breathing legacy of a lifetime at war.

In such a lifetime, Aethon has experienced his share of shocks and surprises. The Corona Chasmi, the dread wonders of Twelve One-Forty-Two. The greenskins of the Gantessa Deeps...

The orks of that pocket empire had grown huge in their iso-lation. As the warp storms around it had cleared, the xenos abominations had reached out from the Deeps to claim the Mechanicum-held worlds of the Melior Corpus.

Aethon would have lost his life to one such giant, but for a Word Bearers Chaplain named Kurtha Sedd. It had been on the frozen forge world of Melior-Tertia, sixty-one years before, that the Ultramarines and the Word Bearers had fought side by side. With the XIII and XVII Legions gathered at Calth to take the fight to another encroaching greenskin empire, Aethon had been looking forward to seeing his friend once more. To perhaps repaying the blood debt he owes the Chaplain.

He will not get the chance now.

The atrocities committed on Calth and the unthinkable treachery hiding in the hearts of the Word Bearers is shock and horror enough to make the Corona Chasmi and Twelve One-Forty-Two fade to forgetfulness. The sons of Guilliman will never allow themselves to forget the pain of this betrayal.

Within the soothing darkness of his plate, the captain is a raw wound. With the stunned taking of every Word Bearer's life, that wound is sprinkled with the salt of unnecessary loss. With every Ultramarine butchered, their failing life signs cascading down his optic overlays like a sizzling memorial, Aethon feels that salt rubbed into his very soul. He aches for the loss of every fallen Ultramarine, as well as the lost legionaries that stand in victory over them. The Legions have become entangled in one another's tragedy and despite the confusion, the hatred and fury of the battlefield, they are both the victims of some greater catastrophe.

The Ultramarines, even with their drill, their theory and simulation, had been blind to this darkest of possibilities. Something, however, has opened the Word Bearers' eyes to that which they should not have seen, and Lorgar and his sons have given themselves to the horror of tomorrow, to a vision of fraternal destruction and blood betrayed. Aethon and his Ultramarines now find themselves in such a vision, fighting for their lives.

The captain wants to roar, to curse and grieve. To shake the shock of this atrocity from his being and feel whole once more. But he cannot. While he hurts for the Emperor's flesh desecrated and his home world betrayed, he cannot allow such weakness to show. His brothers – both Word Bearers and Ultramarines – will hear the adamantine edge of Guilliman's voice in his own. They will feel the Emperor's wrath in the thunder of his shot and shell. They will know the certainty of war everlasting.

Aethon feels his hearts slow. Battle and bloodshed seem to ebb about him, as though Calth itself has ceased to turn. Light fades all around. The Veridian star dims and then grows in eye-searing intensity. Like a waxing and waning eclipse, the sun appears to be suffering some cataclysmic event. With its momentary fading, Lanshear is plunged into the twilight of an unexpected dusk. Seconds later, the sky seems on fire with the sickly brilliance of a false dawn. On the horizon, cutting silhouettes through the smoke, wreckage and clashing legionaries, the rays of Veridia feel their sickly way across the battlefield.

I wish the sun unrisen, the mark turned back, the brotherhood unbroken.

Something precious has been lost. The galaxy was to be ours. Humanity was to bring the light of civilisation to benighted worlds and cleanse the stars of races unworthy. A glorious union of worlds won by those who carried the bloodline of the Emperor

– a bloodline now tainted by treachery. Must we be reminded of truths long forgotten and measures unbecoming? Must we become the Angels of Death to our own once more? Much I fear of this new dawn untrue, for it brings with it more than a new world. It brings a galaxy redefined, a crusade stalled and a kindred foe.

Aethon leans into a murderous turn. He wills the bulk of his Terminator suit around, feeling the fibre bundles contract and servos following his movements. The helm's internal display highlights the blue outlines of Ultramarines lost in a sea of crimson plate and darkness. The battlefield is awash with traitor legionaries, their leering helms coalescing from the murk. Green eye-lenses stare hatefully down the length of boltguns. Chainblades chug, then thrash for the strike.

Aethon does not wish to kill any of them. He has only his primarch's orders, the dire necessity of defence. Thousands of Ultramarines have been slain, but every avenging death takes the Legiones Astartes further from their former union. Aethon does not delude himself with fantasies of control. He has none. Havoc reigns. Death will be the only victor.

As his former allies are redesignated enemy targets, the captain senses a millisecond delay in his combi-weapon, *Moricorpus*. With bolter and melta barrels gaping at oncoming Word Bearers, the weapon's spirit registers confusion.

You give me no choice. Do not test my loyalty.

A Word Bearer dies, then another, and another. Aethon's heart feels numb. His cries of battle are hollow with regret and hoarse with rage. For the first time in his life, the captain feels unsure. It is a seed of doubt, taken root in the pit of his stomach. The Word Bearers seem as sure as madmen can be, throwing themselves at him like deranged beasts. Aethon can't take solace in insanity. All he has are orders, his primarch's orders: *'Defend yourselves by all means at your disposal.'*

So defend himself he does.

Steloc Aethon of the 19th turns his weapon on a crimson-armoured killer. He allows *Moricorpus* its protest before an insistent tug of the trigger punches several rounds into the warrior's chest. As the legionary crashes to the ground, the captain fells two more. Bolt-rounds spark off his reinforced armour like falling meteorites. Aethon will not find his end in the sights of a traitor. His noble plate will not permit it.

More Word Bearers come at him, shouldering through the dimness and the confusion. The ornate decoration of his rank and the bulk of his suit prove an irresistible attraction to his foes.

'Protect the captain!' Aethon hears across the vox-channel, before a volley of bolt-rounds cuts his assailants down from behind. It is an ignominious end for a legionary, but the Word Bearers give them no choice.

Aethon feels the approach of an enemy through his sensors. Turning, he guns the blade of his chainfist. An assault company Word Bearer tries to bury his chainsword in Aethon's shoulder, and the captain smashes it away. The sword sparks and bounces off Aethon's heavier weapon, throwing the traitor back. Bringing the chainfist down with a powerful swing, Aethon cleaves the Word Bearer's hands off at the wrists. As his armoured gauntlets fall to the ground, still clutching the raging chainsword, blood fountains from armoured stumps.

Kicking the Word Bearer back, Aethon returns his grievously injured foe to the throng of advancing traitors. Another chainsword bites into the double-bonded ceramite of his pauldron, and the captain cannot turn fast enough to avoid it. As the blade grinds across his armoured back, Aethon repeats his manoeuvre, striking the sword away with his chainfist before plunging his hand through his enemy's chest-plate.

As the weapon chews through the screaming Word Bearer's torso, Aethon heaves the traitor up before him. Using his foe as a living shield, Aethon soaks up a stream of bolter fire. Turning back on the oncoming Word Bearers, he tosses the corpse free and thrusts the barrels of his combi-weapon at his attackers. Plugging bolt-holes through the throats of two Word Bearers, Aethon takes the head clean off the last with a roaring blast of heat from the melta.

The captain hears the battle cry of a deranged Word Bearers sergeant as the traitor runs up the mound of corpses Aethon has created. Jumping at him, the sergeant swings a jammed chainsword above his head. The buckled weapon bounces off Aethon's plate, but connects with enough force to make him stumble back. Bringing *Moricorpus* up, Aethon fires, taking the chainsword from the sergeant's grip and prompting him to draw a bolt pistol. Again, in a shower of sparks, Aethon takes the weapon – and several armoured fingers – from the sergeant's hand. Bringing the combi-weapon level with his enemy's head, Aethon watches as the Word Bearer stumbles back over a compatriot's corpse, finding himself on the ground.

Aethon strides forwards, stamping down on the bolt pistol before the sergeant can reach for it with his other hand. Stepping across the Word Bearer's body, the captain crushes his gauntlet beneath his heel then brings his boot down on the sergeant's faceplate, crushing the Mark IV helm into the dust.

Abruptly Aethon's vision flashes green as blasts of raging

plasma smack into his Terminator armour. The captain stumbles back in his scorched suit, the photonic blaze crackling and melting the ceramite, leaving smoking craters in his pauldron and breastplate. Aethon bellows in agony as another shot seethes through the heavy-duty cabling of his plackart. The plasma bubbles through his side with the heat of a star and the captain staggers and howls into the vox.

His warriors smash through their foes with renewed urgency, making to support Aethon. Releasing the trigger of the chainfist mounted on his arm, the captain holds up a gauntlet to his men. He screws up his face and, with teeth gritted, blinks the worst of the pain away.

My body – like my home world – is afflicted. Pain. I embrace it, as Calth must do also. I make it my own. Only the living are privy to the agonies of existence. The failing of the flesh, the spirit ready to break. The searing ache of hearts that beat betrayed. I suffer as Calth suffers. We live still, and that is no small miracle.

As he opens his eyes Aethon finds his optic reticules tracking movement in the fray. With the sickly rays of the sun intensifying once more about them, casting the battlefield in a shadow-cleft haze, the Word Bearers are disengaging from combat. They retreat, spraying bolter fire in their wake, and Aethon assumes that some local victory has been achieved by the Ultramarines fighting across the Lanshear Belt.

As the light grows with an unnatural brilliance, the captain begins to realise that he could not be more wrong.

'Permission to pursue, captain?' an Ultramarines veteran sergeant calls, but Aethon barely hears him.

Through the criss-crossing of shadows, Aethon makes out the outline of a lone Word Bearer. Unlike his treacherous brethren, he is a motionless silhouette. Green eye-lenses

shine ghoulishly from a crested helm, rivalling the lumi-
nescence of his plasma pistol's fusion core. The pistol's fat
muzzle still smokes with the trailing afterglow of agitated
hydrogen. While a cloak marks the Word Bearer out as a
centurion of some significance, it is the head of his mighty
crozius maul that identifies him as a Chaplain. Having fought
side by side with the Word Bearers, Aethon knows that the
XVII Legion favour many such spiritual leaders among their
ranks.

As he wills *Moricorpus* up, the blazing agony in his side
making the manoeuvre a trial, the Chaplain stares back.
Through the bolt-streaked murk and the withdrawing shapes
of his brethren, he sights along the length of his arm and
the plasma pistol fixed on the captain.

The Word Bearer tilts his helm in curious recognition.

Aethon's eyes widen. *Kurtha Sedd?*

Perhaps it is him. Perhaps it isn't. Through the eye-scalding
radiance that reaches through the battlefield haze Aethon can
barely tell his men from the enemy, let alone Word Bearer
from Word Bearer. But the possibility alone stokes the fires
of fury in the captain's chest. Targeting reticules converge on
the Chaplain as his overlaid outline flashes before Aethon's
eyes. His helm display confirms for a second time that the
target has been acquired and that the Chaplain is in his
weapon's sights.

Aethon holds him there a second longer. A second too late.

With a glowing green wash of highlighted inscriptions rip-
pling across the Chaplain's plate and a throng of retreating
Word Bearers backing through Aethon's line of sight, the
figure is gone.

'Permission to pur–' the sergeant beside him calls again,

the last of his words lost to a blast of bolt-fire that follows their enemies into the ghostly distance.

Aethon is about to answer when his vox-link changes channel to receive a priority communication.

'This is Ventanus, Captain, Fourth,' the vox-stream crackles.

'Yes, captain,' Aethon replies, but as Remus Ventanus's words run on and echo about his helm he comes to understand that all of the Ultramarines are receiving the message simultaneously.

'I am making an emergency broadcast on the global vox-cast setting. The surface of Calth is no longer a safe environment. The local star is suffering a flare trauma, and will shortly irradiate Calth to human-lethal levels. It is no longer possible to evacuate the planet. Therefore, if you are a citizen, a member of the Imperial Army, a legionary of the Thirteenth, or any other loyal servant of the Imperium, move with all haste to the arcology or arcology system closest to you. The arcologies may offer sufficient protection to allow us to survive this solar event. We will shelter there until further notice. Do not hesitate. Move directly to the nearest arcology. Arcology location and access information will be appended to this repeat broadcast as a code file. In the name of the Imperium, make haste. Message ends.'

'Captain?' the sergeant asks. Like the rest of the Ultramarines standing about him on the battlefield, he looks to Aethon. The captain's plate dribbles sparks from where it has been breached. He turns to take in the Veridian sun as he has done a thousand times before.

Today will be different. Everything the light touches will perish.

You mongrels. You aberrant wretches, unworthy of the Emperor's blood.

You've slaughtered my brothers, and killed my world…

'You heard Captain Ventanus,' Aethon says across the vox. 'We seek shelter underground from the wrath of the star. Duty awaits us in the darkness. We shall drive the enemy back into the light and scorch his treachery from the surface of Calth. Go now, for I fear we shall not be the only warriors to dare the depths.'

TWO

ARKAN DARDANUS RUNS. He runs hard, as hard as his powered plate will allow. About him are fields, where dark crops dance in the breeze. The wind is at the veteran's armoured back – the air pushed forth ahead of the cataclysm unfolding behind. It is madness. It is death.

'*I am the fist,*' Dardanus recites, '*clenched tight in ceramite, smashing with the force of a Legion. I am the blade, awaiting my foe's flesh, as keen as the Emperor could make me. I am the bolt, fired from afar – fleet and true, an end to all who stand before the Imperium of Man.*'

The words are not his. They belong, like many good words, to his primarch. Their purpose is to combat confusion with clarity, to banish doubt and reinforce a legionary's purpose. As Dardanus's hearts thunder in his chest, he feels Guilliman with him, urging him on.

His breath howls about the inside of his helm. The servos

and fibre bundles of his suit hiss and sigh with every ground-pulverising step. The agricultural fields stretch endlessly before him. He turns at a run. He cannot afford to stop. Speed is everything. He has even dropped his empty bolt-gun for the second or two it might buy him. About the Space Marine there are others. Ultramarines stragglers, members of Squad Sephirus. Word Bearers running for their worthless lives.

Behind him the glare is unbearable. His helm display crackles and glazes to static. Where the rays of the poisoned star hit the surface of Calth, flames leap for the sky. A radioactive firestorm tears across the planet, turning the ground to irradiated ash. In silhouette form, Dardanus sees his sergeant and squad running before the light. Some help injured brothers limp before the raging Veridian storm. Others slow to exchange gunfire with spent Word Bearers.

Dardanus feels he is being enclosed in a titanic trap. At his heels comes the heat of the encroaching blaze; before him rise the dark mountains and rocky highlands that mark the perimeter of the vast fields.

He hears gunfire. Sporadic, opportunistic, wild: nothing like the sustained staccato of bolters during battle. There is barely time to think, let alone aim and fire, but this does not stop both Word Bearers and Ultramarines damning themselves with their dalliance. Training and instinct are hard to resist, especially for the sons of Guilliman. The Ultramarines are bred for war. It is not in their nature to run.

But the warriors of Ultramar have never fought a *star* before, and they recognise the futility of it.

Bolt-rounds cut through the crops, blasting heads from stalks and thudding into the rich earth. The Word Bearers ahead aren't even trying to hit the Ultramarines, they are merely trying to slow them down. Dardanus has no desire to engage them. He pushes on at full speed, his only desire to reach the arcologies before the Word Bearers arrive in number and deny the Ultramarines entry.

'All warriors of Ultramar understand what it is to fight and to win,' Dardanus mouths within his helm. 'Victory, however, is more than just a state of mind, more than the choice of weapon and foe. It is spatial. It is temporal. It is sensitive to the vagaries of time and place. An Ultramarine must know where and when it is best to fight.'

Across the open vox-channel, Dardanus hears Brother Galen die. The sound breaks his recitations. There is an oath, a scream and then a blast of static as the tainted star claims another battle-brother of Squad Sephirus. Dardanus remembers years of fighting beside Urius Galen in the primarch's name – the purging of Twelve One-Thirty-One, the crash of the Invictron, hunting xenos abominations on Ceresta Secundus. Within moments his battle-brother is gone. Ceramite, flesh, blood – all that Galen was, claimed by the star.

Scaeron is next to fall; he tarries to vent his fury upon Word Bearers who are equally doomed. Ptolemus is next, the heavy weapons specialist slowed down by the extra bulk of his missile launcher.

As Dardanus stamps through the crops, cutting his own path across the colossal field, he passes Lorgar's traitors. Some he finds dead, surrounded by corpses in brilliant blue plate. Others he discovers praying for a deliverance that will never come.

Those Word Bearers who are not streaking ahead and making the most of their head start wait for Dardanus and his brothers among the crop stacks and great, itinerant storage skiffs. Dardanus leans out of the path of hurried bolter fire. Brother Phantor, who has kept pace with him for most of the run, is not so lucky, and dies with a bolt-round in his chest.

Running straight into a pair of waiting Word Bearers, Dardanus slams into the first, shouldering the traitor into the side of a tractor scoop. He gauges the stance of the second, ducking beneath the arc of a sacrificial dagger. He does not stop to face the Word Bearer, instead surging on, priming a frag grenade on his belt and allowing it to bounce in the wake of his footsteps. The detonation rocks the farming machinery and shreds the Word Bearers. Dardanus stumbles with the blast but manages to keep his balance, throwing himself once more into a powered run.

Driving his transhuman body to its limit Dardanus hits a harvest track, a byway for the heavier agricultural machinery. The coordinates sent with Captain Ventanus's final message have guided him towards the nearest arcology complex entrance. He is not the only one with such information, however, and with each pounding step Dardanus is joined by converging legionaries. Ultramarines and Word Bearers run in from all directions, all intent on reaching the underground shelter. Here, on the approach and with the raging fire at their backs, enemy legionaries are heedless of one another.

No time is wasted in the discharge of weaponry or the swing of swords. All that matters is speed.

The same cannot be said for those in the complex itself. In the distance, Dardanus sees a fat tower, an ancient fortification that marks the entrance to the arcology system. Gunfire rages about a cleft nestled in rocky foothills below it, an advertisement to all of the contested location. Here, at the foot of the tower, Word Bearers and Ultramarines battle to secure the position for themselves and their respective Legions.

A stuttering stream of enemy bolter fire forces the veteran to slow. Dardanus can hear Brother Tibor and Brother Solarius gaining behind, with Sergeant Salvatar Sephirus bringing up the rear. Tibor returns merciless fire, his expert marksmanship ripping through one of the Word Bearers even at a run and sending the traitor flailing back into his compatriots.

'Keep going!' Sephirus barks, the exertion of the run and the furnace roar of the Veridian lightstorm equally audible across the channel. 'To tarry is to die.'

'We're not going to make it,' Solarius says, his voice hoarse.

'We *will* make it, brother,' Sephirus shouts back. 'We will march, run or crawl for Macragge if we have to – for to doubt yourself is to doubt the strength of the primarch. The strength that boils in your blood for the wrongs done to our brethren this day. Now move yourselves, for your Legion, for Guilliman and for your Emperor!'

As rocky foothills turn to carved structures and the gravel track gives way to flagstones, Dardanus sprints for the arcology entrance. Sculpted columns in the cracked rock line the narrowing approach, closing like a gauntlet and funnelling arriving Space Marines down towards the gaping entrance at the base of the tower. Dardanus can hear the armoured boots of Tibor, Solarius and his sergeant behind him.

The entrance is chaos. Ultramarines and Word Bearers make use of what cover they can find, working their way back towards the doorway in tight groups. Bolter fire flies amid the ancient architecture and criss-crosses the entrance approach in furious streams.

Dardanus runs on, pounding his way through the madness. Exhausted, he wants to crash to his armoured knees. While they are still outside, they are vulnerable. With Salvatar Sephirus urging what is left of his squad on, Dardanus and his brothers keep up the pace. They hammer their way down between the columns, just ahead of a similar group of Word Bearers. Streams of bolts cut across the open space while Word Bearers and Ultramarines tangle hand to hand in armoured clashes, pushing each other back and forth through masonry and dilapidated architecture.

Dardanus flinches as a bolt-round glances off the side of his helm. He can see the arcology entrance, a broad, stone arch held by a pair of Word Bearers. Another backs under the archway, retreating from the deadly brilliance of the stellar storm and joining his fell compatriots.

Taking cover within, the traitors send a hail of bolts at anything blue that approaches, but with the unnatural blaze closing, the Word Bearers struggle with their aim and the identification of targets. More than once, Dardanus sees the enemy gun down the silhouettes of their own brethren by mistake. Above them, the thick metal blast door slowly trembles shut, the vault's automated systems closing off the arcology entrance in response to the unprecedented changes in temperature.

Dardanus hears a grunt across the vox and the sound of a bolt-shell punching through one of his brothers.

'I'm hit!' Solarius calls. Dardanus turns. They are so close, but so is the Veridian brilliance, razing its radioactive way towards them. Solarius doesn't even get chance to slow as a Word Bearer steps out from behind a half-smashed statue of Roboute Guilliman and back-swipes the Ultramarine's head from his shoulders.

'Go on!' Sephirus roars, blasting the Word Bearer aside with the last of his ammunition. Dardanus and Tibor do as they are bid, sprinting for the closing vault door.

Running through a storm of shells, the Space Marines about him have allowed their proximity to the entrance to lull them into a false sense of security. Falling back pillar by pillar and wasting their last moments on desperate, vengeance-fuelled wrangles, Word Bearers and Ultramarines alike underestimate the firestorm fury of Veridia. Dardanus can feel the monstrous heat through the plate on the back of his legs. He will not make the same mistake.

The veteran runs straight at a Word Bearer picking himself up off the ground. An Ultramarines sergeant lies at his feet, one of many armoured bodies strewn about the arcology entrance. The Word Bearer puts a final round from his bolt pistol through the sergeant's head before turning his weapon on Dardanus.

Dardanus doesn't even try to engage the traitor, instead using his speed and exhausted momentum to smash his shoulder into the Word Bearer, knocking him back off his feet. Dardanus staggers and tumbles also, but somehow he keeps going, half-running, half-lurching towards the closing vault door. Brother Tibor is right behind him, kicking the bolt pistol from the fallen Word Bearer's grip.

Dardanus accelerates towards the closing door. The metal is dun and pitted with age but the tainted brightness of the sun is such that its brilliance glares back at him from the blast door's shuddering surface. At this range even the blinded Word Bearers cannot miss.

'Let your intentions be as dark and impenetrable as the void,' Dardanus recites – his primarch's words on his dry lips. 'But *when you strike, do so like the plummeting meteor – an unstoppable force that rains fire and shakes the enemy to their core.'*

Dropping, Dardanus skids down onto the entrance floor. Sparks sizzling from the plate on his leg and elbow, the Ultramarine slides through the corpse-strewn entrance. With bolts blasting above him, Dardanus snatches a boltgun from a dead Word Bearer before rolling in under the thick metal door.

Skidding to a stop and thanking the Emperor for the bolts left in the magazine, Dardanus hammers several rounds into one of the Word Bearers. As another turns his boltgun on him, the Ultramarine blasts the traitor in the throat, sending him stumbling back. The Word Bearer clutches at his neck with one gauntlet and pumps bolt-rounds wildly about the arcology vestibule as he falls. Dardanus rolls across the curvature of his breastplate. The Word Bearer covering the other side of the archway already has the Ultramarine in his sights but his boltgun *clunks* empty. The Word Bearer drops it and reaches for a pistol. The crimson gauntlet never reaches the grip of the side-holstered weapon, however, as Dardanus puts what is left in his own boltgun up through the traitor's faceplate.

'Arcology entrance… cleared of enemy targets,' Dardanus reports across the vox, barely catching his breath. As Brother Tibor jumps Dardanus's prone form and takes position by the archway side, the door trembles towards the floor.

'Make haste, brothers,' Dardanus hears Salvatar Sephirus call. It is difficult to make the sergeant out against the firestorm glare, as the brilliance of the afflicted sun embraces Lanshear, the fields and the bordering mountains in its blinding annihilation. Approaching warriors are reduced to eclipsed, shadowy suggestions. Brother Tibor puts down any whose burning green eye-lenses identify them as the sons of Lorgar. Several Ultramarines stragglers make it inside, including Brother Vantaro of Squad Sephirus, whom Dardanus had given up for dead.

Crawling through armoured corpses, Dardanus pats down plate to find a spare magazine. Slamming it into the traitor's boltgun and priming the weapon, Dardanus remains on the ground, taking aim. He can make Salvatar Sephirus out – just. The sergeant is pinned down behind a column by Word Bearers backing towards the arcology entrance. With the boltgun kicking in his grasp, Dardanus cuts the traitors down.

'Vault entrance clear, sergeant,' Dardanus reports.

Salvatar Sephirus makes a break for it. All is shadow and light. As the sergeant makes a dash towards the entrance, however, he falls. Out of the furious brilliance steps a throng of Word Bearers. An enemy sergeant steps over Sephirus, whose bolt-ridden pack sparks from where the traitor has blasted him in the back. The Word Bearers sergeant draws his fist to his armoured chest and salutes his Ultramarines opposite in treacherous mockery.

'Damn you all,' Sephirus spits as the Word Bearers stand over him, their boltguns pointing down. With his pack shot and power to his plate's automotive functions cut, the sergeant might as well be lying in a sarcophagus.

As the Word Bearers sergeant turns and stands before the shuddering blast door, the Veridian firestorm raging up behind him like a towering wall of flame, Dardanus holds him in his sights. No words are needed. The Word Bearers have Sephirus – and they want in, exchanging the sergeant's life for their own. As they point their weapons down at

Sephirus in silence, the Ultramarines holding the archway take their cue from Dardanus, holding both their boltguns and their enemies in place. Dardanus hears his sergeant across the vox.

'There is no victory…' Salvatar Sephirus says.

'…without sacrifice,' Dardanus answers, completing the recital.

'Dardanus,' Brother Tibor says. There is no more time. The new dawn is upon them.

'Sever the hydraulics to the blast door,' Dardanus orders.

Tibor turns his boltgun on the monstrous pistons, and bolt-rounds shred the baroque piping and archway controls. The Word Bearers sergeant and his men break into a run. As the colossal weight of the vault blast door drags it towards the floor, Dardanus watches both the Word Bearers and his squad sergeant melt into the blaze and brilliance.

'Burn, you traitorous dogs,' Dardanus says, 'in fires of your own making.'

Like a clap of thunder the blast door smashes closed, shaking the rocky vestibule and raining grit and dust down on the Ultramarines. The boom of armoured fists can be heard on the door exterior, accompanied by screams and the furnace-whoosh of Veridia's ferocious fire. Within the Ultramarines' helms, the vox-channel cuts to static.

Brother Tibor moves over to Dardanus and helps him up. The Ultramarines stand there. They are numb, in shock. The betrayal, the star, the death of Sephirus. They give each other the blankness of their helm lenses. Something unspoken passes between the squad members. Dardanus nods slowly. As the longest serving battle-brother in the squad, it is down to him to lead. There is expectation; there is protocol.

In the distance, deeper in the arcology tunnels, the Ultramarines can hear the furious exchange of bolter fire – legionaries both crimson and blue, who reached the arcology complex before them.

'Tibor,' Dardanus says, 'try and raise our brothers. All channels. Captain Ventanus. Aethon of the Nineteenth. Anyone. An officer to whom we can pledge our strength.'

'Aye, brother.' Tibor doesn't mean to address Dardanus with such deference but it feels natural the moment the words pass his lips.

'Vantaro,' Dardanus says, above the roar of the stellar storm against the blast door. 'Welcome back, brother. Move on into the outer complex. I need numbers. Who's trying to take control of this section and can we do anything about it?'

Brother Vantaro salutes him, before pounding away down the statue-lined vestibule.

'Brothers,' Dardanus says, addressing the remaining Ultramarines, passing his gaze across their myriad squad and company designations. 'Ammunition is sparse. Collect magazines from sons of Guilliman who have given all they could.' He pauses. 'And search the traitors too.'

As the Ultramarines fall to the task, the blast door booms. Tibor and Dardanus exchange glances. Dardanus does not know how, but seemingly someone is alive out in the radioactive maelstrom roaring beyond the door. As the Ultramarines aim their boltguns at the door, Tibor reaches out, placing his gauntlet against the metal. A second quake prompts him to draw back.

'Get back,' Dardanus orders. 'Secure the entrance.' The Ultramarines take their positions about the blast door, making use of bolt-scarred architecture as cover.

As Dardanus steps back, his boltgun aimed at the thick metal of the colossal door, the impossible happens. With an excruciating scrape, the blast door begins to creep up, allowing crackling brilliance and roaring flame to roll in through the widening gap. Dardanus stares as the door rises, inch by inch, admitting the inferno of the poisoned star. It is hard to believe anything could survive the absolute annihilation and wrath of Veridia. Dardanus promises himself that the interloper – if an enemy – will not survive the wrath of the Ultramarines.

THREE

[mark: 24.46.31]

SERGEANT ORESTRIAN URCUS knows only the punishing brilliance of the Veridian star. Within his suit of Cataphractii Terminator armour he suffers the intimate cacophony of alarms and klaxons. The layers of ceramite that form his reinforced plate and protect him from enemy and environment alike are melting. Bathed in the lethal radiation of a poisoned sun, the Tactical Dreadnought suit is operating at its limit, protecting Urcus from the worst of the radiation and the roasting heat.

Nothing stops Urcus. Not Calth's crashing oceans, not the mountains that carve up the seemingly endless expanse of fields, not the fathomless depths of the spider-haunted caves and arcologies. Proud, like a towering titanwood, he stands above his squad, commanding a silent respect. Legionaries look up to him because they have to. He batters them in the practice cages. He smashes their records. He decimates their enemies on the battlefield. He is not sergeant by choice, for Ultramarines like Urcus – hailing from the salt of Calth's fertile earth – have no need for the respect that goes with rank. He is sergeant because the cold, killing power of his presence on the battlefield demands no less.

As a Terminator sergeant, he surrounds himself with a host of other slow but deliberate killers. Ultramarines who loom over their brothers in their Cataphractii suits, and who are brought in to pulverise the enemy like a battering ram when the formalities of tactical deployments and codified manoeuvres fail to generate the results they should.

Urcus takes one step. The another. Then another. The Cataphractii suit, with its extra weight, plate and resilience, restricts his speed. As Captain Ventanus's order came across the vox, Urcus and his squad had to watch Word Bearers in their pitiful plate run for their lives – and run they could, leaving the Cataphractii in their dust. Urcus had cursed them for cowards. Before the order was given, there had been the satisfaction of enemy slaughter. The same satisfaction that came of a hammered fence post thudding into the ground or the tumble of towering crops before the scything blade.

Urcus lets his officers and primarch afflict their heads and hearts with dark considerations of betrayal and vengeance. Across the vox, the sergeant hears Ultramarines swear oaths of revenge and threaten their former brethren in the XVII Legion with sword and boltgun. Urcus will have no such indulgence among the veterans of his own squad. He knows what he is – all he is. He has long accepted the fact that he is a weapon: a means to an end.

Before Urcus came to serve Guilliman, his family served Ultramar as strongbacks, toiling in the fields of Calth so that

the empire might eat. It mattered no more to Urcus that his
enemies were now Space Marines than it had when his kin
moved between enclosures to harvest a new crop. The Word
Bearers were not the first to fall short of the Emperor's expec-
tations. All flesh was grist destined for the mill.

In this respect, the Emperor's Space Marines were no different to ordinary men. Some were not destined to realise
their purpose – to stand tall before the reaper's blade and be
cut down in their prime. Some were weak. They bent before
the wind and allowed themselves to be taken by the canker.
It is simply Urcus's duty – as it had been his family's on the
Calth of long before – to sort the blighted from the bounteous. Instead of chainscythes, a pair of lightning claws crackle
at his sides. Instead of sentinel-harvesters trudging up the
endless rows, squads of Cataphractii Terminators stalk the
churned earth, cutting down the Urizen's golden sons with
boltgun and blade.

Urcus blinks sweat from his eyes. It rolls down his face,
tasting salty on his lips. The temperature outside has super-
seded his suit's ability to regulate it. He is now relying upon
the fortitude of his own flesh and his engineered advantages
to resist the penetrating power of heat and radioactivity.

In the raging maelstrom that swirls about him, the immaculate blue paint of his plate peels away to the black of
scorched ceramite. Rivulets of melting material dribble down
the armour's sticky surface and sizzle to flame as they drop
to the ashen floor.

The sergeant's auto-senses blink moments of blinding
inferno between intermissions of overloaded static. Squinting, he can barely see where he is going, although the
indomitable progress of his armoured footfalls takes him

ever onwards. Ventanus's instructions carry with them the coded locations of the arcology entrances to which all Ultramarines are directed. Urcus, like his blinded brothers in their Cataphractii plate, trudges towards the promise of one such shelter.

Urcus relies not on encouragement or brave words, for he has none. A simple soul, at heart, the sergeant favours action over words. What good are words, and indeed the precious resource of wasted breath, to an Ultramarine who falls before adversity? Better to save such breath and conserve strength wasted on empty passions. Better to fortify the resolve and demonstrate through action what can be achieved. Urcus will simply lead, and the strongest will follow.

As he marches through the fury of the star, each step a back-breaking trial and with his reinforced suit melting about him, Urcus remembers a work song from his family's toils in the fields. A memory of his early youth, plucked from the rush of thoughts racing through his heat-addled mind. It feels a long way from the shock, the horror and the suffering of the Word Bearers' atrocity.

Over our heads is ol' Veridia,
She's on our back all day,
Why don't you go down, ol' Veridia,
Let the darkness have its way.

Urcus sees shapes in the blinding fury beyond – warriors in crimson plate, stumbling about in the blaze. Lurching through the radioactive firestorm, his foes bump into him, reaching out for the scorching surface of his armour. The sergeant sweeps them aside with his claws. He will not deviate from his course. The Word Bearers totter and fall to the razed earth, their armour and bodies erupting into flame.

As his vision crackles from static to the horrific reality of being burned alive, Urcus barges his way through screaming enemies, flames swirling about them all. While the torched Word Bearers crash to their knees to burn as flame-ravaged husks, the sergeant staggers on – only the thickness of his plate saving him from a similar fate.

Over our heads is ol' Veridia, the song plays out in his head.
She burns all fierce and bright,
Why don't you go down, ol' Veridia,
An' let me enjoy the night.

Urcus stomps on. He can hear the screech of his hydraulics and the hiss of fibre bundles driving his failing plate step after dreadful step. Each one is a scalding agony. Across the vox he hears the stifled suffering of his squad as they march indomitably on. Urcus hears the crash of plate as small mountains of ceramite hit the sun-sizzling stone beneath their feet. First Lepidus, then Brother Ephanor fall, claimed by the heat of the furious star. There is no going back for their flame-writhing corpses, locked up in the metal coffins of their Cataphractii suits.

A Word Bearer shrieks pleading renunciations before Urcus, appearing out of the fiery brilliance like a phantasm. One moment he is flesh and plate. The next he is a slurry of liquid tissue and melted ceramite, swept up in the stellar storm and spread across the scorched blackness of the sergeant's suit. As the cinders and ash of the enemy whirl away with the fire, Urcus glimpses something behind them. For precious moments, static cuts through his auto-senses before the systems momentarily recover to reveal the metal of a blast door. It dances with flame. Taking several agonising steps towards it, the Terminator sergeant hears a boom as his staggering suit collides with the thick metal. He lurches back and almost falls – which would have been a death sentence in the firestorm eating its way through his plate.

'I… have located… the entrance,' Orestrian Urcus announces to his squad. He can barely draw breath in the heat of the suit. 'It is… closed.'

Dropping down onto one knee, Urcus wills his lightning claws to crackling intensity. Punching forth with all the strength he has remaining to him, Urcus buries the claws in the stone at the foot of the blast door. He hauls upwards, runs the blades through the shattering stone until they sink into the metal of the door. The lightning claws slip a little way into the metal before locking against reinforcement struts running through the blast door's structure.

Urcus heaves with his arms and pushes up with his legs, his limbs burning with effort even under the servos of his armour. The sergeant pulls on everything he has left. Every hour spent in training comes back to him. Every hour spent cutting his exhausted way through xenos abominations and enemies of the Imperium. Urcus tries to think of anything else but the pain coursing through his breaking limbs. Anything but failure. If he drops the door now, he will never be able to get it back up.

Over our heads is ol' Veridia,
Please don't make me beg,
Why don't you go down, ol' Veridia,
It's time to go to bed.

Urcus feels the systems augmenting his already formidable strength giving way. Fibre bundles grind and pop. Sparks flash within his helm, causing him to screw his eyes shut. Finally, he feels the door rise. He is winning the battle against gravity.

'Get… in,' the sergeant manages, holding up the blast door, his suit buckling under the weight. The devastated Terminators duck under the bottom of the door, bulky silhouettes against the lethal brilliance that accompanies them in.

Urcus turns beneath the weight of the door as the last of his Cataphractii stagger in. The palm of his lightning claw squeals against the metal. He thrusts the blast door upwards with the last strength his body and suit have to give. Bathed in the full blinding brilliance of the Veridian sun, Urcus finds that he cannot catch his breath. It is like being hit with a wall of light. The blaze is everything. The sergeant knows that his arms and the warping servos of his Terminator suit could give way at any moment. Stumbling in, he pulls his claws out from under the blast door, allowing it to thunder back to the ground.

Suddenly the light is gone. And the heat. And the terrible pain. All Urcus knows is the boom of the door, reverberating up the rocky vestibule of the arcology complex entrance. Grit scrapes beneath his boots as he drags one around and then the other. His limbs feel like molten lead, hot and sluggish. He crashes down on his knees. Squad Urcus stand still about him, their blackened, paintless suits smoking like statues recovered from a fire. Dust and ash from the closing door billows about their armoured forms.

As the tortured systems of the sergeant's plate begin to recover, his auto-senses sizzle back to standard spectra. Overlays warp and cut out before attempting to re-establish themselves. All the suit has for him is a scrolling list of damaged sensors and plate integrity warnings. As the dust clears, the display is able to reinstate targeters and scanners. The sergeant's auspex tells him immediately that he isn't alone.

He hears a tap against the back of his helm as the muzzle of a boltgun drifts in to nestle against it. In the haze, Urcus picks out the shape of Ultramarines in suits of Maximus power armour. Taking cover behind pillars, statues and ancient architecture, they have the smouldering Terminators in their sights.

Urcus realises the danger of his predicament. The firestorm from which he has walked has stripped the paint, regalia and markings of his plate, leaving behind a scorched and steaming surface of ravaged ceramite. For all these other Ultramarines know, the dust-wreathed Cataphractii belong to the Word Bearers. It dawns on Urcus that he and his squad might have escaped the wrath of Veridia, only to be executed by their own brothers.

The Ultramarines veteran at his back moves around, his boltgun aimed squarely between the Terminator sergeant's eye-lenses.

Exhausted, Urcus tries to speak, but his throat is bone-dry. A strangled whisper barely registers on the vox. He tries again but the extended silence of systems restarting and the sergeant's inability to identify himself makes the Ultramarines increasingly suspicious. They lean in with their weapons.

'Hold,' a voice says, clean and crisp across the vox. Moving up the sloping vestibule, accompanied by a power-armoured veteran, is Aethon, captain of the 19th Company. 'Lower your weapons,' the captain commands. Aethon carries himself awkwardly, a sparking crater in his side leaking blood down his belt tassels and the plate of his right leg.

Keeping their weapons trained on Urcus, the Ultramarines turn to see the approaching captain, then lower the muzzles of their boltguns. The veteran before Urcus points the barrel of his weapon at the ground before turning to present himself to the officer. As he does, Urcus reaches out for the veteran's pauldron with his lightning-clawed gauntlet. Hauling himself up, the Cataphractii Terminator almost drags the other Ultramarine to the ground. Urcus leaves his claw on the veteran's shoulder, partly to inconvenience him, and partly because the spent Terminator has to.

The power-armoured veterans slam their fists against their chests, saluting the captain of the Honoured 19th.

Where the other Ultramarines see a captain, though, Orestrian Urcus sees a friend. While Urcus's family had been toiling topside in the fields – farmhand strongbacks, moving with the seasons – Aethon had been raised as the son of an underworld castellan in the principal arcology of the Gallica Subdelta. The pair have little in common but in calling the world of Calth their home. Both found a new home in the ranks of the XIII Legion, however. Being recruited together. Training together. Serving together as Scouts, battle-brothers, veterans and Terminators.

Aethon had always been destined for glory and advancement. He had always been articulate and complex, a serious young man with a love of his duty, his Legion and his world. When such devotion was rewarded with a return to Calth to help Roboute Guilliman turn the planet into a multi-levelled fortress worthy of Ultramar, Urcus had accompanied his captain.

'Sergeant,' Aethon says, his voice grim and formal. He knows his friend by sight, even after being delivered from the hellish fires of the tainted star.

'The White Spider,' Urcus returns, managing the words before breaking into a parched cough.

'I haven't heard that name in a long time,' Aethon tells him, his tone softening.

'Nobody knows these underground labyrinths better than you,' Urcus says. 'Not even the things that creep and crawl and make this tomb their home.'

'Knowledge of the arcology complexes might be the only advantage we have down here,' Aethon tells him.

Urcus coughs again before recovering himself. 'Since when have we needed an advantage?' The pair fall easily into the banter of old friendship, like a plough finding the furrow.

'It's good to see you, Orestrian,' Aethon tells him honestly. 'I only wish it were under less dreadful circumstances. It has been a dark day, with an eternal night to follow. I will need your help.'

'I'm yours – as always.'

'Our last count indicates almost half of the Legion lost,' the captain continues. 'What Ultramarines made it to the arcologies are scattered, along with their praetors and officers.'

'What of Guilliman?' Urcus asks. 'What of the other captains?'

'For now we are cut off from Legion command and each other,' Aethon says. 'The primarch lives but the fleet has been forced to withdraw. In all honesty it could be many months before we see reinforcement or evacuation. Perhaps years. The captains? I don't know. Ventanus can't be far. Tetrarch Nicodemus was fighting up from Komesh. Phelion of the 44th was fighting with me across Lanshear – but I'm pretty sure he's dead.'

'He is,' Urcus confirms.

'This is our fight now. A war that has taken to the shadows.'

'I'm an Ultramarine,' Urcus says. 'I fight where my primarch needs me.' While Aethon speaks with the lyrical steel of an educated man and a born leader, Urcus can't help but approach the grim reality of the situation with blunt determination. It is their way. It always has been.

'I would expect no less of you, friend,' Aethon says.

'What of the enemy?' Urcus asks. While Aethon's grief strains the delivery of his words, the sergeant will not sentimentalise the XVII Legion. They are a foe to be destroyed now and they always will be.

'Treachery has nestled between their hearts for a long while, brother,' Aethon seethes. 'They flood the arcologies in great number. I'm gathering what battle-brothers I can to secure the doors and outer complexes. I'm going to drive the enemy back. Down into the lower levels. Down into unfamiliar territory, where we'll drown them in the darkness.'

'The turncoats will adapt.'

'Which is why we must hit them hard,' Aethon agrees. The captain turns to the power-armoured veteran standing beside his friend, the Ultramarine who had been about to put a bolt through Urcus's head.

'Name?'

'Brother Dardanus, captain,' the veteran answers.

'Brother Vantaro here tells me you secured this blast door,' Aethon says, indicating the Ultramarine in power armour who had accompanied him up the rise.

'Yes, captain,' Dardanus reports. 'We lost our sergeant in doing so.'

Orestrian Urcus takes his mighty claw from the veteran's pauldron.

'Stand straight,' he tells him. ' You're about to receive an honour.'

'I'm promoting you to acting sergeant,' the captain tells Dardanus. 'It is the first of what I expect will be many field promotions this day. Take these battle-brothers as the beginning of your new squad. I will fortify your numbers as soon as I have the men to spare.'

'Thank you, captain,' Dardanus says. He glances briefly at Urcus. 'As the sergeant indicates. It is an honour.'

Aethon turns and walks back down the vestibule slope, towards the gunfire of the Ultramarines he left securing the chambers below and beyond. 'Gather what munitions you can,' he calls back, 'and prime your close-combat weaponry. We shall need to save bolts where we can, and that means a good deal of close fighting against an enemy that our codifications have ill prepared us to face.'

'Yes, captain,' Dardanus says, stripping the last magazines of ammunition from the bodies of the Word Bearers who were silent witnesses to their conversation from the vestibule floor.

'Yes, captain,' Urcus echoes, trudging down the slope with his Cataphractii brothers, their mauled plate still smouldering. Ammunition stripped, Dardanus falls into line with his own Ultramarines.

'Are you all right?' Urcus asks, drawing level with his captain. Aethon is carrying himself awkwardly in his Terminator armour, compensating for the wound in his side.

Aethon says nothing at first. 'I think,' he confesses finally, 'that it was Kurtha Sedd.'

'The Chaplain?' Urcus asks, casting his mind back to days of xenos eradication on distant Mechanicum factory worlds, some sixty years before. 'From Melior-Tertia.'

'Kurtha Sedd,' Aethon repeats absently.

Urcus grunts a grave acknowledgement. He knew Kurtha Sedd, but not as Aethon knows him. Unfortunately, the sergeant has no comfort for his friend. Urcus comes from a world of stoic acceptance. Aethon, meanwhile, hails from a background of advantage and possibility, where problems are not endured but solved.

Urcus knows how much it must pain his brother to call Word Bearers like Kurtha Sedd enemy. He is a warrior of whom the captain has always spoken with warmth and honour. In the cavernous vestibule, however, the Word Bearer's name echoes horribly, the now wretched syllables carried away by the serpentine twist and turn of labyrinthine passageways.

FOUR

THEY CALL CAPTAIN Aethon the White Spider, and Arkan Dardanus can see why.

Days follow. Days of desperation, hatred and blood. The arcology tunnels are overrun with Word Bearers – warriors of savage fanaticism. Trapped between the Ultramarines and the depths, the traitors fight hard. Cut off, like the Ultramarines, from their own command, they are like animals free of the leash or cage. Territorial, they make the darkness their own. Caverns. Sub-level storage depots. Arcology vaults. Pipelined conduits.

They are everywhere, vomited forth from the depths. Lying in wait, like traps of armour, madness and death-pledged flesh, their only desire to slaughter innocents and lay low the sons of Guilliman. The captain, however, is fearless in the face of their atrocity. Aethon's fury can be heard in the serrated edge of his battle cries and the cold disbelief of bolter

fire. The order of the day is death, with swords, chainblades
and throttling gauntlets leaving a trail of dead Word Bearers
in the Ultramarines' wake. Armoured corpses of brothers,
stripped of ammunition and left to rot.

The White Spider forges on, sending the Space Marines
of his limited force north, south, east and west. He sends
them to secure the outer complexes and the maze of tunnels that extend level by level below. To networks clotted
with cavern depositories, pillar-reinforced arcology chambers and operations nexi. Like a crooked web, extending
in all directions, Captain Aethon lays claim to subterranean territories infested with the enemy. He sends his
avenging emissaries out through the underworld, driving
back the Word Bearers and taking Calth back one piece at
a time. Where the Lorgar's faithless sons think they have
found shelter from the surface they find only death, in
the form of righteous warriors purging the depths with
bolt and blade.

'Update your records,' Aethon tells his rag-tag group of
sergeants, as the officers stand about the simplicity of a
map etched into the rock of the chamber wall. With suit
lamps dancing across it, the map shows the main arterial
routes reaching across and down through an area called
the Arcology Perpetuis. The map is unhelpful, bereft of
labels and the detail of sub-networks. The captain fills
many of the gaps from memory, talking through his plan
to clear areas of enemy contingents, secure them and seal
them off with control-fused section doors and engineered
collapses.

Dardanus waits as the White Spider gives his instructions.
Sergeant Urcus towers nearby in his sun-scathed plate, the

captain's shadow. Ultramarines sergeants and acting sergeants who have been given command of depleted squads
receive their orders. Scouting missions. Instructions to
explore, take and hold installations of value. Orders to
clear sub-arcologies of Word Bearers or take their turn
as part of the vanguard force, driving the enemy from
improvised positions, gauntlets and ambush-points in
the main arcologies. Like Dardanus, each of these sergeants has served in such a capacity, their buckled and
gore-spattered plate telling unspoken tales of unending
murder and ferocity.

'Acting-Sergeant Dardanus,' the captain says, scraping the
ceramite tip of his gauntlet across the map. 'This arterial
dragway leads to a blister of vaults here. It's known as the
Proprium-Termini, a storage facility. Take your squad and
reconnoitre the facility for enemy forces and anything we
can use. Report back with your findings.'

'Yes, captain,' Dardanus says. He leaves the gathering to
recall his squad from the cavern beyond. Other sergeants
are ahead of him, leaving with their men, the echo of their
armoured footsteps full of grim determination. Behind him
he hears Aethon despatch others. Galtarion and his men are
sent to deal with a Word Bearers sergeant they have come to
know as Maldreq Fal. Fal, ghoulishly announcing himself
and his dark loyalties to Lorgar Aurelian through the twisting tunnels, has somehow worked around the Ultramarines
advance with his brethren and is harassing the force's rear.

Ulantus Remulo gets the honour of a cleanse and burn mission through the Gordia Warrens, while Sergeant Tynon and
his Terminators are assigned to relieve what's left of Dromedon Pax's men at the vanguard.

Crossing the cavern, Dardanus passes through a sea of besmirched blue plate. Ultramarines all, of different squads and designations: exhausted, injured and ill at ease. Hour by hour they are discovered, fighting alone in the dark for their lives or working their way through the underworld of Calth in tight groups, intent on pledging themselves to an Ultramarines officer as Dardanus had.

Sometimes their vox-transmissions make it through the static of stellar disturbance. Sometimes they announce themselves with a hoarse challenge to the shadows of approaching legionaries. Outnumbered, low on ammunition and stunned at the betrayal of their legionary brothers, they arrive or are discovered in a sorry state. Every single warrior of Ultramar is welcome, however, and all find new purpose in the White Spider's bottomless drive and determination.

Dardanus nods to brother Ultramarines as he moves through their number. Some are warriors he is familiar with. Others he barely recognises through the blood and fury on their faces. They hide their pain behind the smashed faceplates of helmets pulled down and locked into place. It is time to spill the blood of brothers once more. Their sergeants are calling.

While Cataphractii Terminators were receiving the attentions of their brothers, field-patching plate and re-routing power cabling, Ultramarines veterans have finished wounded Word Bearers off, taking magazines from their belts and individual bolts from their weapons. Grenades are a rare and valuable find, but Aethon has instructed his legionaries to scavenge anything they might find useful in the taking of enemy life. The Ultramarines, already a vision of savagery in their blood-splattered and bolt-pocked plate, now carry belts that are a mag-locked nest of recovered combat blades and notched short swords. Hanging on straps from the nodes of their packs are smashed and recovered weapons – partly functional plasma guns, battered meltas and all-but-empty flamers. Anything that will kill the deserving.

Grievously injured Ultramarines receive the benefit of medical supplies scavenged from within the arcology. Those bearing the extra burdens of shredded plate, bolt-blasted knees and broken limbs have been designated as ammunition carriers. Moving between their brothers with their bolt pistols during vicious firefights, they allocate precious magazines from stockpiles of recovered munitions slung in webbing carry-alls. The combat-ineffective are sent back to the upper levels, where Aethon instructs them to wait with the citizens of Calth.

Having benefited from Captain Ventanus's broadcast warning, reaching the arcologies with both Ultramarines and Word Bearers, the sun-scarred survivors of Calth are scattered throughout the upper arcologies. Some have even taken to the depths for safety but they find only monsters there – traitorous madmen who find use for their screams, their sacrifice and their souls.

Those that hid for their lives reveal themselves to the advancing Ultramarines like ghosts bleeding from the darkness. They bear the mark of Veridia on their dust-smeared faces and the blank stares of the horrified and the lost. The captain gives them all he can at this time: which is honesty, brutal and cold.

He tells them that there will be a time for survival and a time for rebuilding – a time when the Space Marines

of the Emperor might be more to them than the distant
thunder of gunfire. Now, he says, is a time for war. Now
is a time for vengeance and the righting of wrongs in fire
and blood. He sends them to be with others of their kind,
to share in their sorrow and find comfort in their growing number. There, Ultramarines who bear the horrendous
price of their brothers' treachery have instructions to watch
over Aethon's hollow people. They will be safe – for a Space
Marine of the XIII Legion is worth more moments from his
death than a thousand men in their prime or a hundred
of Lorgar's turncoats.

'Squad Sephirus,' Dardanus says, prompting his Ultramarines to rise wearily, gathering their helms and weaponry.

'Perhaps that should be Squad Dardanus,' Iolchus Tibor
suggests, trying to raise the mood.

'I am but acting sergeant,' Dardanus tells him, attempting to
muster a glimmer of appreciation in his eyes before pulling
his helm down. 'We shall save that honour for another day.'

'Day?' Saraman Aloysio mumbles. He looks about the cavernous gloom. 'Night, you mean. All the people of this world
shall ever know is the perpetual night of these depths, for to
look upon the sun is to know darkness forever.'

Dardanus gives the Ultramarine the blankness of his
eye-lenses. Brother Aloysio is not one of his veterans but
upon reaching the arcology blast door became one of his
squad. He has the haunted look of those formerly of the
Librarius, although Dardanus would never press him on
this matter.

'Move out,' is all the acting sergeant has for him. 'Your
heading is east by north-east. The arterial dragway.' He allows
Tibor, Vantaro, Aloysio and the rest of the squad past, leaving

Hadriax with his heavy bolter and a newly acquired limp to bring up the rear.

As the squad leave the cavern, they find at the dragway entrance an Ultramarines sentry who salutes them with a clenched gauntlet to his chest.

'Vantaro, on point,' Dardanus orders. He thinks on his captain's words. 'Be the tip of the spear, and spare not the traitor before its thrust.'

'Aye, sergeant,' Vantaro replies, leading the way with his suit lamps and boltgun. Young for his assignment to a veteran squad, Vantaro has the eyes of a swooping Imperial eagle and the aim to match.

As the squad files down the dreary length of the dragway, their lamps bouncing around the walls, they present their boltguns, though they have little intention of using them in all but the most desperate of circumstances. As Dardanus sidles down the bored-out tunnel wall, looking back and forth, he comes to realise how perfect the dragway would be for an ambush.

His Ultramarines move around a handcar hanging from the rails that run the length of the dragway ceiling. The car is laden with storage crates, that upon inspection contain sundries and dry goods.

'Squad Sephirus, this is Command. Report status and position,' the vox crackles, struggling even with the short distance between the dragway and the cavern. The speaker is Brother Medon, the captain's nominated communications officer.

'Acknowledged, Command. Squad Sephirus advancing down the dragway, east by north-east. Coming up on the storage vaults. No contacts.'

'Command out.'

As the monotony of the tunnel length begins to take its toll, Dardanus's thoughts run once more to his primarch.

Who more than you, great Guilliman, must feel the torture of a brother's betrayal? The XIII and the XVII share a legionary brotherhood. We are distant and as different as two Legions can be. Still, it wounds me as much to thrust a blade into a brother as to receive one. What the Urizen has done – to you, to the sons of Ultramar, to Calth – must be a thousand blades, forever in the stabbing. To the fortitude of your flesh, your heart and your mind, afflicted as it is with questions unanswered.

How could Lord Lorgar – a primarch himself, bearer of the Emperor's word and gene-sired of his precious blood – have brought us to this? To have spilled his brother's blood from legionary veins. To sully more the forgotten history of this Great Crusade. How could his sons have so easily, so completely turned on their kindred? Where is the strength of their engineering? Where is the nobility of their calling? For bolts crafted for the abominable races of the galaxy have been put to ever more terrible use. To slay warriors and their brethren. Will the galaxy ever be the same again? As Guilliman teaches us, 'For empires to find peace they must first know war.' I don't think even the primarch considered that we would be fighting ourselves.

'Targets…'

Dardanus slows, grit crunching beneath his boots. It is Vantaro across the vox, his voice hushed. Cycling through his visual spectra, the acting sergeant sees that Vantaro has stopped some way ahead, assuming cover behind several metal barrels stacked at an alcove waystation.

'Halt,' Dardanus orders calmly. The Ultramarines stop in unison. 'Assume cover formation,' he tells them, prompting Squad Sephirus to move to the tunnel walls. They each lead with their boltguns in one gauntlet and clutch stabbing blades in the other. Dardanus advances at a crouch, cursing the powered sigh of his suit as he makes his way up to Vantaro.

As he kneels down beside the barrels, Vantaro points at the chamber beyond. Through the false-colour of his helm display, Dardanus makes out a cavernous storage depot. Small mountains of crates, barrels and cargo caskets dominate the chamber. Some have been arranged on metal pallets and wrapped in plastek webbing, while others are giga-containers the size of tanks.

Dardanus doubts any of them contain weapons or munitions. Those container stamps he can make out indicate preserved foodstuffs and canistered water. Little use to the Ultramarines in the prosecution of their solemn duty of death and destruction, but invaluable in the establishment of the camps and protectorates that will inevitably follow.

As Captain Aethon has predicted, the identification plaque at the chamber opening reads 'Proprium-Termini'. Casting his gaze across the chamber Dardanus sees huge units of curling machinery built into the rock of the far wall, quite out of place with the prosaic nature of the depot. The units throb in their dormancy.

'What do you make of that?' Dardanus asks, indicating the machinery.

'Power generators?' Vantaro guesses.

'That's a lot of power for a storage facility,' the acting sergeant muses.

'Whatever it is, it's interfering with my auspex readings,' Vantaro says, prompting Dardanus to check his own.

'I've got static,' he confirms.

'It's your decision,' Vantaro says.

'No,' Dardanus corrects him. 'It really isn't. The captain wants this facility reconnoitred and we can't do that from here – especially with scanner interference.' He changes his vox-channel. 'Command, this is Squad Sephirus. We've arrived at designated destination. Proceeding with our sweep.'

'Acknowledged,' Brother Medon returns, his voice a warped crackle.

Dardanus switches his vox-channel back. 'Squad, quarter and search by twos. Be advised – we're getting auspex inter-ference from the stellar anomaly. Rely on sight and sensors only. Proceed.'

The Ultramarines move through the cavernous storage facil-ity. As they routinely sweep left, right and behind with their boltguns, the warriors make their cautious way down the crooked rows of the Proprium-Termini. Even their careful steps cause tiny quakes to pass through the towering col-umns of stacked cargo. Dust cascades about them from the tops of crates and giga-containers.

'Nothing,' Tibor reports, reaching the end of his row with Brother Laertus.

'Vantaro?' Dardanus says across the vox. Like Tibor, the sergeant has encountered little beyond pump-trolleys and poorly stacked cargo.

'A valuable find, sergeant,' Vantaro tells him. 'Supplies – many months for many people.'

'Munitions?' Dardanus asks. He already knows the answer. He is being thorough.

'Little of note,' Hadriax confirms, drifting the bulk of his heavy bolter around. A belt of bolt-rounds dangles from the weapon, indicative of what little ammunition the

Ultramarines carry with them after the demands of the battle on the surface. 'Certainly nothing worthy of an Ultramarine. Some survey charges. Deep core seismic detonators. Mining demolitions, bearing the markings of the Pioneer Corps.'

'Worthy or not,' Dardanus says, 'lay markers for their recovery. No opportunity is to be wasted. The captain may find use for them and beyond that, they must be denied to the enemy. Brother Aloysio: the mechanism?'

Aloysio and Brother Eurymachon stand before the colossal power units built into the rough rock of the facility walls. Eurymachon looks down the scope mounted on his boltgun, covering Aloysio, who investigates the machinery.

'Definitely power generators,' Aloysio tells him. 'But supplying this much power, down here, they must be–'

The dormant reactors suddenly roar to life, filling the cavernous chamber with their cacophony. The thunder builds swiftly in stages, while power crackles across the pipes, vents and nodes of the units. An excruciating sound follows, proceeding from further machinery hidden in the rock behind the reactors, then a dirty flash of light.

'It's a blast door!' Brother Eurymachon reports, identifying the source of the light. He moves with Aloysio down the wall of machinery to stand before a large alcove. Within is a closed bulkhead. Eurymachon brings the muzzle of his bolter up to the armourglass slit set in the door while Aloysio attempts to peer through the soot-smeared glass.

'Can't see a damned thing,' Aloysio says.

Then, like the first tumbling pebbles of a rockslide, the Ultramarines hear it. Squad Sephirus spin around with the reflexes of engineered warriors. They pivot and lean into the presented death of their weaponry. There is little their boltguns can do to stop what is happening. Mountainous stacks of cargo are collapsing. Canisters, seal-caskets, metal crates and great giga-containers tumble down towards them. The angular bounce of their ugly descent displaces further stacks, dragging entire columns of cargo down with them.

Dardanus and his men try to back up, but the avalanche of crates and canisters engulfs them.

The acting sergeant shoulders containers aside and shrugs off the impact of smaller pieces of cargo. He can hear the shriek of Brother Laertus's chainsword beside him as the Ultramarine attempts to deflect the weight of bouncing canisters out of his path in showers of sparks. A giga-container falls lengthways before them, booming as it hits the depot floor, before toppling over to land upside down. Pushing Laertes out of the way, Dardanus throws himself back, allowing the crate to thunder down between them.

Vantaro isn't so fortunate. Dardanus hears his stifled scream as another giga-container tumbles, riding the collapsing cargo before rolling straight over him. Clipping Hadriax also, the colossal container goes on to smash into the wall, disgorging its contents across the floor.

Then comes the gunfire from above. Word Bearers hiding amongst the cargo, lying in wait before heaving the small mountains of supplies down on the unsuspecting Ultramarines. Turning their hiding place and existing claim of the Proprium-Termini into an ambush.

Sound is everywhere – the roar of the machinery, the metallic boom of tumbling crates and spilling containers, the harsh crack of boltguns. It is difficult to think, let alone act, but Dardanus cannot afford not to. A battle-brother stumbles through the settling cargo, clutching his neck. He has taken a bolt-round to the throat, his grunts and choking filling the vox. He takes several more in the chest and pack from Word Bearers shooting from the towering stacks, before a round to the temple puts the Ultramarine down.

'Take cover,' Dardanus orders, trying to keep his voice even. He kneels down before a canister of consecrated oils but bolter fire shreds the container, fountaining its viscous contents all over the ground. Slipping and staying low, Dardanus moves from cover to cover, the Word Bearers' merciless fire chewing through crate after battered crate. 'Hadriax: suppression fire.'

Hadriax is not the only Ultramarine to be firing. Eurymachon's weapon barks single bolts up the slope of collapsed containers, while Tibor's economic blasts take apart a Word Bearer who has toppled with the cargo. Hadriax has recovered from the impact of the giga-container and is dragging the broken Vantaro to shelter inside it. From the warped doorway of a colossal crate, Hadriax unleashes his weapon. Heavy bolter fire plucks through the slope of demolished cargo, tearing crates into the air and punching through webbing-lined stacks. As the gunfire tears across the top of the cargo columns, Word Bearers retreat behind cover, allowing Dardanus to reach a small mound of shattered crates.

'Door opening,' Aloysio announces, backing to one side of the alcove entrance. Both Aloysio and Eurymachon have avoided the worst of the collapse. As soon as the doors shudder hydraulically apart, however, the darkness beyond is lit up with flame. Eurymachon is in mid-turn, bringing his bolt-gun from targets in the stacks around to the opening door. Staring down the scope, all he can see is his own fiery doom.

As Brother Eurymachon is blasted away by a broad stream of flame, a squad of Word Bearers in battered crimson plate proceeds from the opening door. They immediately make use of cover in the form of the crates and canisters strewn across the depot floor and the baroque bulk of machinery lining the reactor wall.

As the sun-scarred Word Bearer with the flamer stops to adjust his primer, Aloysio comes up behind him. The Ultramarine hasn't been seen and makes the most of his opportunity by plucking a curved blade from the traitor's belt and stabbing it straight through the side of his bleached helm. Relieving the Word Bearer of his flame unit as he falls, Aloysio disappears behind a booming wall of fire that swallows up the squad rearguard.

The air comes alive with the fresh discordance of bolter fire, tearing through the cargoscape and turning crates and their contents to shrapnel. Dardanus knows he must act fast. Squad Sephirus must prise the jaws of the sprung trap back open and fight their way free.

'Tibor, Laertus: support Brother Aloysio with the arrivals,' Dardanus orders. 'Hadriax – I need covering fire on the stacks.'

As Hadriax sweeps his heavy bolter back and forth, his gunfire ripping through the top of the stacks, Dardanus leaps out from behind the mound of crates. With the Word Bearers forced to take cover from the heavy bolter, Dardanus follows the crash of gunfire up the slope. Holding his boltgun against his pauldron, the sergeant claws his way up the incline of collapsed cargo with the other hand.

Blasts of opportunistic bolter fire proceed from the newly arrived squad of Word Bearers, one round almost knocking

Dardanus off-balance as it strikes his pack. With the whoosh of a flamer, the shriek of Laertus's chainsword and the sharp crack of Tibor's precision marksmanship, the slope-mauling streams of gunfire are redirected, allowing the sergeant to continue his ascent.

Gripping tightly with his gauntlets, Dardanus hauls himself up the side of giga-containers, crates and the tangle of webbing. Amid the crashing of Hadriax's heavy bolter, the sergeant hears the clatter of something bouncing down the slope towards him. He guesses what it is before the grenade rattles past him. As it disappears down between the side of a giga-container and the cargo half-burying it, Dardanus attempts to scramble away.

The dull thud of the detonation crumples the container and throws the contents of crates and barrels up into the air. Flung away by the muted force of the explosion, Dardanus ends up on his back, some way across the slope. With debris raining about him and loose cargo kicked away by his scrabbling boots, the Ultramarine attempts to right himself and brings his boltgun in close, nestling the weapon against his pauldron. He rolls over and points the boltgun up the slope to the precipice from which the giga-container was originally pushed. The Word Bearer who lobbed the grenade is there, looking back at Dardanus down the length of his own weapon. Both tug back on their triggers.

Dardanus looses off a short burst of bolts up at the crimson-clad traitor, taking him through the faceplate, and watches as his foe tumbles back and down the slope with a clatter of plate. Dardanus climbs, punching his gauntlet into the demolished pile of cargo before clawing his way up. All the while he keeps his other arm outstretched, his boltgun aimed at the top of the other stack.

As heavy bolter rounds thump into the mountain of disgorged crates, the Word Bearer taking position there retreats, turning his attention to Dardanus surmounting the parallel stack. Instead of an easy target, he finds the hollow invitation of the acting sergeant's muzzle waiting for him. Holding himself taut and in place, Dardanus crashes several rounds through the Word Bearer.

As the traitor collapses to his knees, Dardanus begins to slip back down the tumbling slope of supplies. The Word Bearer's death is quiet and sombre. No oaths or curses. Just a legionary on his knees, allowing the last of the transhuman life to drain from his body.

Satisfied that the Word Bearer is dead, Dardanus finally pulls himself up atop the cargo stack. Claiming the first Word Bearer's ammunition, the sergeant risks standing. The stack feels unsteady. Below him the battle unfolds. Word Bearer and Ultramarine, faceplate to faceplate. Throttling. Kicking. Bludgeoning with fist and boltgun. Stabbing and spilling guts with the shrieking blur of chainsword teeth.

Among Guilliman's sons gunfire is sparse and largely reserved for the certainty of the kill. They understand the strategic demands of the war to come. The Word Bearers blast their weapons with zealous abandon, as though they care not for the inevitability of boltguns run dry. Dardanus dreads to imagine what other weapons the traitors have at their disposal.

Dardanus runs across the top of the stack, launching himself for the second. The mound of demolished stores and containers shudders with the impact, prompting further cargo slides. He climbs the half-buried webbing and pulls himself up.

As his helm rises above the top of the stack, the Word Bearer on his knees seems to come to life. Drawing back, Dardanus realises that the traitor is not reaching out for him but has merely fallen forwards under the force of bolt-rounds punching through his pack and into dead flesh. Thrice-cursed bolts meant for Dardanus's head instead tear through the stack top and the Word Bearer's armoured corpse from the next stack along.

The sergeant hears the unmistakable *thunk* of a heavy bolter reaching the end of its belt feed. Hadriax has no punishing cover fire left to offer him. Dardanus doesn't have time or ammunition for a protracted engagement. Reaching up, the sergeant depresses the magazine stud on the dead Word Bearer's boltgun. Taking the half-empty magazine, he sees also the grenade mag-locked to the traitor's belt. Slapping the clip to his own weapon, Dardanus pulls the grenade free, just as another savage bust of bolter fire erupts from the far stack to maul the crimson-plated corpse.

Dardanus primes the grenade. He makes his estimates. Distance. Height. Descent. Throwing the grenade up above the stack and into the darkness of the storage cavern roof, the sergeant waits. And waits. He intends the weapon to strike the top of the stack as it detonates, but never knows if he hits his target. From the far side of his stack Dardanus hears the thunder-crack of the grenade's detonation. Half a heartbeat later there comes a second, then a third and a fourth, heralding a sequence of cacophonous booms. The cavern's craggy ceiling is briefly bathed in explosive illumination. Stalactites tremble and fall. The stack on which Dardanus is perched collapses beneath him, knocked over by the force of the blossoming detonations ripping through the chamber.

Everything is a vertiginous tumble. Dardanus feels himself rolling with the avalanche of cascading cargo. Tangled in webbing, his armoured elbows smash crates flat. His plate is baptised in drinking water from ruptured metal casks and his helm bounces off the side of a toppling giga-container. He clings to his boltgun like some sacred relic, unwilling to let the tumbling crates and storage containers knock it from his grip.

Finally coming to rest on the chamber floor, Dardanus finds himself buried in cargo. He takes a moment to collect his jangled thoughts. The grenade must have set off further munitions – the mining demolitions, or the seismic charges. Clawing himself free of the cargo webbing, Dardanus erupts from the sea of debris covering the depot floor. The cavern still rings with the ear-splitting roar of subterranean detonations. He rights himself with difficulty, finding Brother Tibor at his side, hauling at the inside of his elbow.

The collapse has taken him down into the desperate battle below. Squad Sephirus, along with the enemy force blasting their way from the alcove, have been swamped by the cargo of the collapsing stacks.

Tibor kneels in the spilled contents of a battered giga-container, firing off single bolts that smash through the helms of Word Bearers attempting to stand in the jumbled mess. Brother Laertus stumbles before Tibor's arc of fire, prompting Tibor to raise his boltgun. Laertus has fought well but has paid a bitter price for his valour. His own chainsword still chugs but the pauldron above is a tooth-chewed mess where a Word Bearers Assault Marine has chopped down through the Ultramarine's cobalt-blue plate and through his shoulder. The flesh and plate of Laertus's arm are barely attached.

Saraman Aloysio, meanwhile, fights like a warrior possessed. The battle-brother is covered in blood, but little of it seems his own as he staggers across the uneven ground to pounce on the last of the Word Bearers ambushers. What Brother Tibor cannot do with his boltgun, Aloysio accomplishes with a scavenged sacrificial athame clutched in one fist and a broad combat blade in the other. The Word Bearer has lost his boltgun in the tumbling melee of cargo that swept him from his feet and is wading towards it.

Aloysio reaches him first, however, burying the athame in the Word Bearer's pack. Using the enemy blade to drag the Word Bearer away from the boltgun and around, Aloysio rips it free and turns himself. He slams both the sacrificial knife and the proud combat blade into his foe's chest, then tears them back, with a screech of metal, from the embrace of the Word Bearer's breastplate. The foe roars his pain and defiance but the heavy combat blade passes in a glinting arc through his throat. Aloysio is splattered with further gore as the Word Bearer topples over, crashing forwards against the Ultramarine's armoured chest.

Aloysio shrugs the dead enemy off, allowing the athame to fall onto the cadaver-strewn mess of cargo and supplies. Wiping the combat blade on some matted webbing, Aloysio mag-locks the blade to his belt with a metallic *clunk*.

Dardanus makes his way with difficulty through the collapsed cargo, crushing crates underfoot and getting his boots caught in webbing. The quiet of the Proprium-Termini has been shattered by the destruction of the Space Marines' fight.

Broken storage containers and their contents lie everywhere. Beyond, the power reactors built into the rock face still hum and the blast doors the Ultramarines have discovered gape open. Mixed in with the slew of cargo at the acting sergeant's feet are the bodies of butchered Word Bearers and a number of Squad Sephirus' own.

'Aloysio,' Dardanus says, his words a metallic hiss through his helm grille. The Ultramarine does not respond. He stands over his last foe, his plate dripping with enemy blood. 'Brother Aloysio.'

'Yes, sergeant,' Aloysio says, dragging himself back to the moment.

'Strip the enemy of their munitions,' Dardanus orders. 'Then clear a space for our fallen.'

'Yes, sergeant.'

'Hadriax,' Dardanus voxes. 'See what can be done for Vantaro and Laertus.'

'Aye, sergeant.'

'Tibor – with me,' Dardanus says.

Tibor doesn't respond, but follows his sergeant across the mess towards the open blast doors.

Boltguns up, the pair move in on the alcove opening. A broad corridor extends beyond, busy with industrial machinery and cloaked in a heavy metallic-hued steam. Surrounded by the throb of the reactors, auspex readings are meaningless. Dardanus feels blind without the scanners, the cost of such loss apparent in the depot chamber beyond. To compound the tension, the sergeant's weapon feels light, his bolts almost spent. Two recovered magazines sit on his belt, almost as empty.

Giant machinery hums about them, filling the air with a

rough static that sizzles across the surface of the Ultramarines' plate. Tibor moves on ahead, his pack to the pipes that line the short corridor leading from the blast door. As he reaches a bend, he silently darts his helm around the corner. Nothing, only more corridor that he carefully negotiates, moving across to the other wall. Dardanus takes his position on the corner, covering Tibor with his boltgun. The sergeant watches Tibor move around trolley rigs and hydraulic derricks, his careful steps a light tap on the metal floor. With boltgun up he advances on the chamber into which the corridor opens.

Dardanus spots the danger first. A flash of crimson plate. The dull glint of a boltgun levelled around the chamber corner. As a Word Bearers sentry leans out to blast Tibor, Dardanus empties his own weapon of its last few bolts. Blasted back, the enemy convulses, dropping his weapon. Round after precious round punches through his chest.

Moving across the corridor, Tibor kneels down beside the body of the dead Word Bearer. He takes in the chamber in which the traitor was standing guard.

'Sergeant, you should see this.'

Dardanus moves up to Tibor and the dead sentry, and the pair strip the corpse of ammunition. Tibor recovers the magazine from the Word Bearer's weapon and Dardanus takes another from his belt. The Ultramarines stand and walk on into the pipe-lined chamber. It is large, boasting stacked barrels of coolant and a sheltered cabin of thick metal and armourglass. The floor and ceiling of the chamber are dominated by thick, dark metal discs that are mounted facing one another.

'Is that...' Tibor begins.

'A teleporter?' Dardanus says. 'I think so. These reactors are certainly powering something down here,' he confirms, checking the empty cabin from which the sentry had appeared. The sergeant's mind fills with the tactical possibilities such an installation could offer. These hopes soon become clouded by the danger it could present in the form of Word Bearers reinforcements. The traitors have already attempted to ambush the Ultramarines in the storage chamber and had brought in fresh men to catch the squad in a crossfire. 'Cover the translation pad.'

Assuming position in the cabin doorway, Brother Tibor aims his boltgun at the teleporter pads. Dardanus leaves him, taking a few steps back into the corridor and the leaden-grey mist.

'Command, this is Squad Sephirus,' the sergeant calls across the static-threaded vox. 'Command, respond.'

'Acknowledged, Sephirus,' Brother Medon replies finally, his voice a distant, interference-strangled echo in Dardanus's helm.

'Command, we have completed our sweep,' the sergeant says. 'We encountered resistance from a Word Bearers force lying in wait and have sustained casualties.'

'Squad Sephirus,' Medon tells him across the warping frequency, *'we have no squads disposed to support you.'*

'Understood, Command,' Dardanus voxes back. 'We have secured the Proprium storage facility and the supplies contained within. We have also discovered what we believe to be a teleportarium terminus, used formerly to transport bulk cargo across the arcology systems. The Seventeenth Legion have refashioned the technology for combat use.'

Dardanus waits. For a short time there is nothing but the

howl of static and the sergeant is unsure if his communication has made it through.

'*Squad Sephirus, stand by,*' Brother Medon says finally. '*Captain Aethon is en route to your position.*'

FIVE

[mark: 72.11.42]

STELOC AETHON STRIDES into the teleportarium chamber, the footsteps of his Terminator suit bringing their own thunder with them. Behind him comes Squad Urcus: hulking Cataphractii in paint-scorched plate. Two of his veteran Ultramarines are covering the translation pad with their weapons.

'Sergeant Dardanus,' Aethon says, standing before the monstrous machinery of the cargo teleporter. 'This is excellent work. The storage facility and now this.'

'Securing the Proprium-Termini was not without cost, captain,' Dardanus reminds him. Aethon detects something in his voice. It is not the first time he has heard it in the reports of his men. Since the atrocity, the patrician accents of Ultramarines – usually so clipped and direct – seem edged with anger.

There is a burr to Dardanus's words, left there by loss. Aethon decides not to engage the sergeant in this. Necessity. Duty. Orders. They are all the Ultramarines have left in the face of wanton butchery and brotherly betrayal.

'You will receive replacements for your lost men,' Aethon tells him, 'so that you may continue your good work in the primarch's name.'

Sergeant Urcus trudges over to the cabin to inspect the installation controls.

'Sergeant?'

'Teleportarium terminus,' Urcus confirms. 'Civilian grade, used initially to transport mining equipment and then for the mass movement of cargo. The depot beyond is no doubt a waystation.'

'Can it work for us?' Aethon asks.

'It worked for the Word Bearers,' Dardanus says, interrupting Urcus. 'Apologies, sergeant.'

'Go on,' Aethon tells him.

'An enemy squad proceeded from this installation,' Dardanus informs him, 'and the Word Bearers left a sentry.'

'Urcus?'

The Terminator sergeant does not sound convinced. 'This installation is designed to transport inanimate equipment and supplies. Shipments probably stray all the time.'

Dardanus comes forward.

'Captain,' the veteran says, 'if I may. The cargo that came through this installation must have been redirected from another teleportarium. This is but a terminus and perhaps there are a number of them, but they must all receive their translations from an installation hub or nexus.'

'I have seen such installations before,' Aethon agrees.

'The Word Bearers clearly hold one of these installations,' Dardanus says. 'I say we use the teleportarium to mount an attack. It will be our best chance to surprise them.'

'We could be walking from one trap into another. Such an installation will likely be heavily guarded by the enemy,' Urcus advises. 'But if you materialise kilometres away, buried in thousands of tonnes of rock, the welcome you would have received at the hands of the Word Bearers will seem like paradise.'

'Still,' Aethon says, 'it seems too good an opportunity to pass up. How many such opportunities can we expect, sergeant?'

'We have no astropath, no homers–' Urcus urges.

'It must be a single-channel system,' Dardanus tells him, 'with the terminus and the hub nexus serving as homers for one another. No guidance is required. We shall simply be returning to wherever the Word Bearers reinforcements came from.'

Aethon considers their options. Urcus remains silent. The Terminator sergeant has made his case, and Aethon knows of old that his friend is not one for deliberation. Dardanus, meanwhile, looks up to his captain. Newly promoted. Keen to impress. Eager to take the fight back to the enemy nest for brothers lost in the depot and on the surface. None of these necessarily make him wrong.

'Sergeant Urcus,' Aethon says. 'You are probably right. But if we are walking into an enemy trap, then there is no one I would choose to be at my side over you.'

'Brother...'

'Captain...'

Aethon knows what they are going to say. Knows that

they will even quote great Guilliman himself if they have to. *For the Emperor stands behind his sons as the primarchs behind their captains. It is a captain's duty to place legionary lives in harm's way before his own. There is too little glory in the galaxy to go around and officers must be generous in the trust they place in others – for one day such brothers must be captains too.*

Aethon understands the tactical sense of his primarch's words – but Guilliman at their speaking had not seen Calth destroyed. He had yet to live the horror of his brother's treachery and knew little of the underground war to be fought in the depths of the decimated planet. There was more at stake here than just martial protocol and codification. Besides, it hurt Aethon too much not to fight. He would fight for his life, as he had asked others to do, on the front line. He would cross that line and tear the heart out of an enemy he had known once to be honourable and true.

'Sergeants, please,' Aethon commands. 'Spare me your protests. Emperor knows, I know the arguments. Sergeant Dardanus: you trust this equipment and this plan. We in turn trust you. What is left of your squad will hold this installation for our return. You will secure it against an enemy counter-attack. If Word Bearers return in our stead, you are to destroy them, destroy this installation and rejoin the main force under Sergeant Phaelon. Do you understand?'

'Yes, captain.'

'Sergeant Urcus, if you please,' Aethon says.

'Mount the pad,' Urcus orders his squad, 'and prepare for translation. Pattern Dentica. Protect the captain.'

As the Cataphractii giants of Squad Urcus lumber forwards, Aethon gestures Dardanus towards the metal cabin. Standing on the great metal pad and with another mounted on the chamber ceiling, seemingly ready to crush them, Aethon assumes position. Urcus will not allow his captain to translate into battle without protection and surrounds him with Cataphractii battle-brothers: a wall of thick ceramite and the presented barrels of combi-bolters, complete with barbed chain-bayonets.

Over the pauldrons of two Cataphractii, Aethon watches Dardanus – who had been so certain of his plan – now examine with uncertainty the heavy-duty controls of the depot teleportarium.

As the deep thrum of the power reactors rises to an excruciating sear, compensating for the extraordinary demands of the bulk teleporter, Aethon primes his combi-weapon. Chambering the first bolt of a fresh drum magazine and activating the pyrum-petrol injection system of his melta, Aethon hears Urcus order his squad to ready their weapons alongside him, before the sergeant's voice is almost lost in the torturous sound of great mechanical industry. As the shriek of the power reactors builds to a skull-splitting intensity, the teleportarium thunders with the engagement of dematerialisation energies. He can hear Urcus again, bawling orders across the vox and above the noise.

'Open fire on my mark! I want fire arcs established as we materialise. Don't wait for the completion of transference…'

As the great machinery of the Proprium-Termini establishes an immaterial integrity about the Ultramarines and their battle-scarred suits of Tactical Dreadnought armour, a metallic mist fills the chamber. Dardanus and his squad inside the cabin are lost to them, as are the barrels of coolant and the pipe-lined walls.

The captain's visor display dies. Aethon closes his eyes within his helm and gives himself to the dreadful sensation of teleportation. He wills his hearts to slow and his racing mind to clear. He feels the exotic forces of immaterial transference tearing at his body and soul. It feels like falling a very great distance, except Aethon is falling in every direction at once. Rather than the minutes it would take to plummet from orbit to the ground, Aethon experiences the abyssal plunge as a single, horrific, everlasting moment.

Thoughts mingle one into another, like wet paint on a remembrancer's canvas. Aethon becomes pain. The ache of his genhanced frame pushed to its physical limit. The wound that still rages in his side, quietly bleeding a mess inside his chafing plate. The dull torment in his heart – the blade of treachery that turns in his chest with every unnecessary death. Every brother, Word Bearer or Ultramarine, who has perished. He feels once-proud Calth about him: its atmosphere a furious inferno of stellar punishments, its fertile earth polluted with the blood of innocents, its stone heavy with the souls of all who had died in atrocity. Calth would forever be a world haunted.

Aethon drifts.

I feel no longer of this world – nor of any other. The glories of my Legion have been eclipsed by the doom of Calth and the dark days to follow. The days spent in butchery below the surface, spent in the hunt for our traitorous kindred. Spent in honouring the loss of Ultramar's myriad sons and the grim rebuilding of our strength and number.

This will come to pass. Those of Guilliman's blood will allow nothing else. And yet, as sure of victory as any Ultramarine has the right to be, something has been lost, never to be regained. Our trials here on this doomed world – my world – mark the dawn of a new and benighted age. Even our future victories will be tainted with darkness and the grave understanding of what will never be.

I ache for a future forgotten but know my place in the bloody present. It is still, however, my duty to find a nobility in the prosecution of such a calling. We cannot become the mindless mirrors of the warriors we fight in the depths. We cannot lose our way in the darkness, as the sons of Lorgar clearly have. I will light the way with the example of action.

Then, everything is gunfire.

Aethon hears the crash of combi-bolters all about him. His gauntlets creak about *Moricorpus* and his chainfist. Opening his eyes, the captain finds Squad Urcus enveloped in metallic mist. The translation plate upon which they stand, and the one above their helms, crackle with immaterial energies that still snake across the surface of their plate. As his helm returns to full functionality, auto-senses give the impression of a much larger chamber. Machinery booms about them. The crackling screech of reactors fades, while the excruciating thunder of the teleportarium grinds down.

Aethon hears screaming – muffled and distant. It proceeds not from the vox or his own armoured warriors: their translation had been successful. The bulk teleporter, rude and unworthy as it was to transport the Emperor's Space Marines, has nonetheless materialised Squad Urcus onto the translation plates of a larger facility, a facility held by Word Bearers.

As ordered, the Cataphractii Terminators are firing with their sergeant. Ultramarines bleed back into harsh reality and the bolts that blast from their weapons become real also, punching through the leaden smog in all directions. As the mists of immaterial transference clear, Urcus calls a halt to fire. Ammunition is precious and must be expended with purpose. About them, armoured silhouettes crash unceremoniously to the deck. Sentries entrusted with securing the teleportarium; sentries who failed in their duty.

'Captain?' Urcus asks.

'Proceed, sergeant,' Aethon tells him. He would not presume to lecture Orestrian Urcus in the arts of war. As the Terminators spread out, thudding bolter rounds into the helms of fallen Word Bearers, Aethon attempts to get his bearings. The teleportarium boasts several exits – maintenance tunnels for the great machinery driving the monstrous teleporter, and sub-depots for storing supplies and equipment. The sound of gunfire doesn't yet appear to have drawn any enemy to their location.

Urcus assembles his squad either side of the main blast door, and peers through the scratched sliver of armourglass that functions as a portal.

'A command nexus?' Aethon asks.

Urcus nods. The sergeant clearly intends to hammer his way through to the installation hub and take the cogitatorium and hardwired communications post belonging to it.

Aethon looks for himself. In the tunnel beyond – a broad corridor of grille flooring and bulk machinery – the captain sees the shapes of Word Bearers taking positions. A throbbing klaxon can be heard beyond the blast door. Aware that they are under attack, traitor officers are sounding the alarm for all available Word Bearers to descend upon and defend the command nexus.

'We don't have much time,' Aethon says.

Urcus nods and hits the control for the blast doors. They rumble ceilingward, with Ultramarines Terminators waiting either side, ready to move. About a third of the way up, the door shudders to a hydraulic halt. The chamber lamps and tunnel lumen globes blink and then fade. The hum of teleportarium machinery dies about Squad Urcus, with even the air circulation systems hissing to a stop. Only the dreadful klaxon can be heard, calling through the tunnels beyond.

'Predictable,' Urcus admits.

'The shadows won't protect them,' Aethon pledges.

'Victurus, Eurotas,' Urcus says. 'Get this door up.'

Standing either side of it, the two Terminators clasp the underside of the door with their crackling power fists and haul it upwards on squealing rails.

'Nereon, Dactys – the honour is yours,' the sergeant tells them, prompting two more of his warriors to step out into the corridor and stomp up along the tunnel walls. The darkness comes alive with the stream of bolt-rounds and the ghostly glow of helm lenses.

As Brothers Nereon and Dactys trudge through the murk towards the enemy, they are hammered this way and that by the impact of enemy fire. Sparks shower from their thick Cataphractii plate as they return economic blasts of firepower. They slog their way up the tunnel, the weight of their suits bearing forwards against the hailstorm of shot pounding them back. On they march, putting one ceramite-encased foot in front of the other, with their captain and sergeant behind them. While battle-brothers in Cataphractii plate in turn step out of line to support with short bursts of fire from their combi-bolters, the two Ultramarines columns work their way up the tunnel.

Aethon hears shouts of alarm and calls for reinforcements. Even in the lightless tunnel, the captain's auto-senses pick out the sizzling, false-colour outlines of armoured bodies. The Ultramarines' bolter fire has found its mark. Word Bearers in their lesser plate have fallen, leaving but two brother-betrayers holding the intersection.

'Brother Pontus,' Urcus commands. 'Let them feel our fury.'

Andron Pontus steps out of line, the scorched nozzles of his heavy flamer ready. The half-empty fuel canister chugs before the intersection is engulfed in a rumble of flame. Aethon squints as the brilliance of the blast momentarily overwhelms his auto-senses. The Ultramarines march on towards the inferno. The Word Bearers stumble through the firestorm, firing off involuntary rounds from their weapons. In the confines of the tunnel there is nowhere for the flames to go and no way for the enemy to escape them. By the time the Cataphractii Terminators reach the razed intersection, the Word Bearers are dead. Amidst the crackle of stone-licked flame they are blasted husks smouldering on the ground.

'Orders, captain?' Urcus says, looking down on the charred remains of their hated foe.

'I want this installation,' Aethon tells him plainly.

'And you shall have it,' the sergeant says. 'Dactys – hold here. The teleportarium is yours. Nothing gets past.'

'Aye, sergeant.'

'Victurus, Nereon, Eurotas – go with the captain,' Urcus commands. 'Brother Pontus, take both your fury and your column that way and clear the section. Brother Hestor, your column with me. We shall cleanse and burn this installation free of our waiting foe.'

As Urcus steps out into the intersection, a stream of bolter fire smashes into his side. He brings up his lightning claw like a shield, the fire of advancing Word Bearers sparking off the crackling talons and leaving blackened craters in his pauldron. The sergeant turns slowly to face the hastily recalled reinforcements. Like an avatar of destruction, he is framed by the dwindling flame of the burning intersection.

The Word Bearers, meanwhile, are false-colour phantoms in the darkness of the corridor, glowing with the blaze of bolter fire. Aethon hears the sergeant's grenade harness *clunk* to priming on his back. A grenade and then a second blast away, flying down the corridor before bouncing along the grille floor and detonating, blowing what's left of the throng of Word Bearers into the rocky ceiling and walls.

'Not a bad start,' Aethon tells Urcus, before striding forwards across the intersection. As the Cataphractii Terminators peel off, the captain leads his men on.

The installation is crawling with enemy: Word Bearers killers and half-squads, lying in ambush. Waiting in the labyrinthine darkness beyond, until the klaxon had called them back. It is they who have been surprised. They that have been caught off-guard. Some remember their training, establishing barricades, gauntlets and bottlenecks for the Ultramarines, trying to check their advance through the installation. Others, like excitable hounds off the leash, come straight at their legionary brothers.

Aethon makes them pay for their lack of self-control. Pushing a barrel of blessed unguent over with the tip of his boot, he kicks it at a crazed sergeant blasting his way around a corner. The rolling barrel puts the Word Bearer down on the ground, where Aethon stands over him before drilling a short burst of bolt-fire from *Moricorpus* through the helmless sergeant's skull. The flowing lines of scripture covering the Word Bearer's face disappear in a flesh-shredding storm of shot.

Bringing *Moricorpus* up, Aethon blasts a second cornering Word Bearer back into the wall and takes the head off a third with a titanic back-swipe of his chainfist. With little for the Cataphractii Terminators accompanying him to do, the battle-brothers stomp past their captain, advancing on the command nexus.

As Aethon approaches, the klaxon gets louder. The darkness is already a cacophony of gunfire bouncing around the twisting perversities of chambers and tunnels. Sparing bursts of bolter fire are punctuated by the whoosh of spreading flame and the glow of distant sections set alight. Over the vox-channel Aethon can hear Brother Pontus calling to his Terminators. Midon Asteriax is dead, while Brother Thasander is pinned down by enemy fire.

About the command nexus, the Word Bearers hold their nerve. Aethon suspects a veteran sergeant is giving orders to arriving reinforcements while his squad stands ready to hold off an attack from an elevated position.

'Captain,' Brother Eurotas calls, stepping over the body of a Word Bearer the Terminator has just clubbed into the floor with his power fist. Aethon moves up behind him. Nereon and Victurus stand within the shelter of a doorway, craning their helms awkwardly around to look up. The vault housing the command nexus thrums with mechanical life and the sound of generator hubs.

Ahead, Aethon can see a towering edifice reaching up through the chamber. The command nexus sits in a nest of lines and cables that snake their way across the grille floor. It stands on a circle of support pillars that run down through the flooring, like a small operations citadel. Cables run from the tower, draping across the open space to interface plugs in the chamber wall before running their hard-lines through solid rock to other installations.

Aethon knows he needs the communications hub and the operations controls that reside within the tower. Casting his gaze up the building, he sees that the only light coming from within emanates from the command nexus at the very top. This no doubt comes from some emergency hololithic display or rune screen that, like the klaxon, received power when all other installation systems had been cut off by the Word Bearers.

The captain's helm display crackles with data. His optic overlays pick out armoured shapes in the darkness, while his targeters drift across the scene. Word Bearers are taking cover behind the pillars upon which the tower stands. Others blast down from elevated positions within the tower itself, including the smashed armourglass of the crowning nexus. Bolts chew up the grille at Aethon's feet and spark off the rocky entranceway, prompting Nereon and Brother Victurus to step back.

Across the vox channel the captain hears Sergeant Urcus

barking orders to his men. Brother Palaemon is dead. Aethon snarls. He is not prepared to waste the lives it will take to lay siege to the tower.

'Brothers,' Aethon says. 'Hold position. Nereon, Victurus – lay down some cover fire for a frontal approach. Eurotas – draw fire from the upper levels.'

Aethon hands Brother Victurus the relic weapon *Moricorpus*. The captain will need both his hands free.

'Brother-captain, where are you going?' Eurotas asks.

'Up that tower,' Aethon tells him.

The captain breaks into a slow and heavy run. Every movement is agony, fuelling his fury further. The damaged cabling in his suit's midriff sparks with the effort and the wound in his side rages with the burning insistence of hurt unhealed.

Aethon accelerates across the vault, bolter fire blazing about him. The Word Bearers are night-sight-filtered smears, momentarily lost in the blinding blaze of their weaponry. Nereon and Victurus do their part, short streams of gunfire drilling into the support columns and forcing enemies to pull back behind cover. As the Ultramarines captain attracts the attention of the legionaries in the tower, bolt-rounds thud through the grille plating about his boots. Aethon feels the impact of bolts on his Terminator plate, singing off his pauldron, pack and helm. As Brother Eurotas's gunfire sprays across the tower, bolters are drawn to the Ultramarines firing from the shelter of the entrance.

As Aethon reaches the support columns, he feels Word Bearers about him in the murk, keen for his blood. They leave the cover of the pillars, confident in their superior numbers as they rush the captain with raised bolters and close-combat weaponry. Aethon hits the nearest foe with the full weight of his hulking suit and the unchecked momentum of his charge. Battering the Word Bearer back off his feet, the captain heaves his chest and helm back out of the path of rounds spat from the presented muzzle of a boltgun. Striking out with the stilled serrations of his chainfist, Aethon turns the barrel aside, sending the staccato of fire into another boltgun-aiming legionary. The Word Bearer doubles over with a grunt of torment and surprise.

Aethon sees the glint of a blade in the darkness, a chainsword hefted overhead by an attacking traitor. The captain brings up his chainfist in an awkward parry, soaking up the chopping impact of the weapon with his arm. As blue bolts of energy crawl along the chainfist, Aethon guns the terrible weapon to life. The thrashing teeth rip the chainblade from the Word Bearer's grip, sending it clattering to the floor. With a roar, Aethon sweeps back with the chainfist. The serrated blur of the weapon cuts down through the armoured torso of the attacking Word Bearer. Knocking the half-cleaved warrior back into the Word Bearer with the boltgun, Aethon smashes that weapon in turn out of his enemy's grip with the raging chainfist.

Aethon slams his fist into the Word Bearer's buckling chestplate, the serrated shaft of the chainfist plunging through ceramite, carapace, bone and engineered organs. The warrior stiffens with shock. Gunning the weapon, the captain mulches the Word Bearer's traitorous hearts before reverse-gearing the chainfist and allowing him to drop.

Turning, Aethon finds two broken warriors before him.

The Word Bearer he charged is now holding himself and his smashed suit up against a support pillar. He tries to bring his boltgun up but a salvo of shot from the Terminators in the doorway puts the turncoat out of his misery. The traitor who received his compatriot's bolts in the stomach can't rise, but his trembling gauntlets go to work on priming a bolt pistol torn from his belt. As the Word Bearer struggles, Aethon strides through the slaughter. Standing next to the doubled-over warrior, the captain hears the Word Bearer curse him in his own rasping tongue.

'This is no more than you deserve,' Aethon tells his enemy. He brings his chainfist to a shrill roar, hovering the blade over the small of the Word Bearer's armoured back, below the pack. Bringing the weapon up and then back down with cold fury, Aethon cuts the traitor in half, spilling guts and gore down through the grille floor.

Looking up at the underside of the tower, Aethon's autosenses probe the darkness of a shaft working its way up through the centre of the building. He can see the underside of an elevator car at the top. Beside the shaft, an emergency stairwell runs up into the command complex. The circumstances seem to qualify.

Turning the door into buckled scrap with a kick, Aethon forces his way through the rockcrete frame of the entrance. Ceramite squeals against the opening but the captain will not be denied. Stomping up the stairs, he feels the stone shift beneath his heavy footsteps. The emergency stairwell was not designed with Space Marines in mind, let alone warriors clad in full Tactical Dreadnought armour. His pauldrons scrape along the walls, the steps crack beneath his boots and the rails bend in the grasp of his gauntlets.

With the Word Bearers holding off not only Aethon's men but also emerging Ultramarines from Brother Pontus's column, the captain hopes that the Word Bearers sergeant and his traitorous brothers holding the tower remain distracted. As bolter fire crashes through the darkness of the stairwell above, he realises that his hopes are for naught.

A door opens, and a Word Bearer peers out with his boltgun pointed down. Gunning his chainfist into action, Aethon punches upwards, ramming the weapon up through the Word Bearer's faceplate and into his skull. Tearing the armoured corpse out of the doorway, Aethon allows his foe to fall down the flights of steps.

The stairwell is both boon and curse. Too small to comfortably admit the captain in his monstrous plate, it is also too small to admit Word Bearers in any number. Sparks flash off Aethon's plate's reactor housing and the hunched hood of his armour as another traitor, two floors up, blasts down at him with a pistol. Heaving his suit around the tight confines of the stairwell landing, Aethon hauls himself up another flight of steps. When he gets to the landing above, he searches for the foe that opened fire upon him.

As he strides through the infernal gloom, the captain's plate is bathed in the red light from cogitator data-slabs running at a low ebb on emergency power. The window is already spattered with bolt-holes from where the Word Bearer has made the most of his elevated position.

Economic bolt-streams crash about the tower as Ultramarines and the traitors of the XVII Legion exchange bursts of fire. His heavy steps hidden amongst the cacophony of the

furious gun battle raging outside, Aethon moves in on the
Word Bearer who opened fire on him.

The traitor hears the final steps of Aethon's careful
approach and turns. He is several heart-thudding moments
too late. As the boltgun comes around, the Ultramarines
captain smashes the weapon to pieces with a savage swipe
of the shrieking chainfist. Grabbing his enemy's helm with
both gauntlets, Aethon smashes it again and again into
the stone of the chamber wall before launching the Word
Bearer through the cogitator banks. Hitting the opposite
wall of the chamber with a sickening crunch, the armoured
figure falls still.

Aethon returns to the stairwell. He is the White Spider
once more.

Hauling. Climbing. Killing. His body aches with the
exertion of heaving his hulking form, plate and all, up
through the emergency stairwell. His chest is hot with the
righteous fury of a Legion betrayed. Such soul-scalding
feeling needs a face. He knows not the Word Bearers he
is killing under his primarch's order. He has never spoken with the dreaded Urizen, in whose name the Space
Marines of the XVII Legion committed themselves to
doom. When Steloc Aethon feels the stone-cold numb-
ness of his Ultramarines betrayed, the bloody necessitude
of Word Bearers blood spilt in earnest or the millions on
Calth caught in between, the only face the captain sees is
that of Kurtha Sedd.

Kurtha Sedd, whose words had been an inspiration and
whose valorous deeds had been an example to Word Bearers and Ultramarines alike on icy Melior-Tertia. Kurtha
Sedd, with whom Aethon had fought side by side against

the common enemies of the Emperor. Kurtha Sedd, who plucked Aethon from the oblivion of an early death at the foetid claws of a monstrous greenskin.

What can Aethon know of the mind of a primarch, or the circumstances that have turned Colchis from the light of the Emperor and brotherly love? But Aethon knows Kurtha Sedd. The captain corrects himself. Knew him.

Where is the man I knew in all of this? The man of wise words and noble deeds. The man who loved his Emperor with a power and conviction that put the sons of Ultramar to shame. What could push a Space Marine of the Legiones Astartes to forsake his empire, his warrior kindred, those whom he might have called friend? Where is that man? How can I tell his darkness from that of those that betray and butcher about him? Can there be anything left of the man I knew in the shadow left behind? The shadow that stalks me across the battlefield and haunts the depths of my dying world?

As Aethon hooks his ceramite fingertips onto the stairwell rail, heaving himself and his heavy plate up the tower, he dispels the notion as a kind of heresy. The order has been given. The primarch's order. The mark has been initiated. He stands at the head of legionary ranks decimated by treachery unrivalled. His armour is awash with traitor blood. There can be no going back from this. Can there?

The vox crackles, a familiar voice broken by the static. *'... captain... closing on your... confirmed...'*

Aethon tries to recall the name of the warrior, but his attention is stolen by the roar of a chainsword, the monomolecular teeth of its blade going to excruciating work on something above. He slows his ascent and peers up the stairwell.

He hears the chainsword's blade chug to idling. The traitor is listening for Aethon's advance.

The voice comes again over the vox, more clearly now.

'Repeat – Captain Aethon, this is Brother Victurus. I am closing on your position. Other squads confirmed as inbound also. Can you give us–'

Sparks fly from the plate of the captain's ruined helm. A Word Bearers Assault Marine stands in the command nexus doorway above. In one gauntlet he clutches the chainsword – in the other a bolt pistol, sending round after determined round down at the Ultramarine.

Aethon roars, stomping his way to the Word Bearer. Rockcrete comes away from the walls and the rail is ripped out of its anchorage by the force with which the captain hauls himself up at his foe.

The Assault Marine swings his weapon wildly. Aethon forges on up at him and turns the idling sword aside with his own chainfist. As both warriors gun their weapons to full, raging speed, sparks shower about them.

The Word Bearer backs through the doorway behind him, the fury of Aethon's attack surprising him. The captain smashes through the doorway, dust and rockcrete raining down about the unaccommodated bulk of his plate.

The pair circle in the extra space afforded by the command nexus chamber.

The traitor has his training and his dark faith. His savage manoeuvres have every right to cleave the captain in two. Aethon meets each thrust and serrated sweep with cutting deflections of his own, smashing the chainsword aside.

Parrying the weapon with his chainfist, Aethon forces the

Assault Marine back. Moving about each other in the darkness of the command nexus, sparks shower the two Space Marines as raging blades clash. Aethon cannot match the Word Bearer for speed. Several times the captain grunts as the chainsword bites into his thick plate. The Word Bearer, however, cannot match the force with which Aethon swings his weapon. The chainfist chops and cleaves with all the augmented strength of the Terminator suit. Aethon smashes the chainsword aside as though it is nothing, following with his clenched gauntlet.

Pummelling the Word Bearer's helm with his armoured fist, Aethon creates enough space between them to land a stamping kick on his enemy's midriff. The Word Bearer stumbles back. He drops his sword, reaching out for the elevator doorway with both hands to stop himself falling down into the darkness of the shaft. Propelling himself back at Aethon with mad fury, the Word Bearer is not daunted by the size and power of the Ultramarines captain.

Moments too late, the traitor realises that he should be.

Snatching his power-armoured foe up in his mighty arms, Aethon hefts him up onto his chest and then above his helm like a training barbell. Pitching the Word Bearer at the nexus window, Aethon sends him flailing through the thick armourglass to fall to his death.

Aethon hears the bark of a boltgun. He feels the rounds impact on his Terminator plate, punching craters into the armour, knocking him forwards. The Word Bearers sergeant has joined the battle, and has shot him in the back. Aethon turns with fury. Across the command nexus chamber he sees a hololithic projection crackle and shimmer before him. It is the faded glory of Roboute Guilliman himself in three-dimensional representation, the pre-recorded message looping over and over.

'*If this broadcast has been triggered,*' says the shimmering primarch, '*a solar event of great magnitude has occurred…*'

Bolt-rounds blast through the projection, sizzling where they pass through Guilliman's noble form before hammering off Aethon's plate. The captain walks towards the hololith, his steps heavy and determined.

Steloc Aethon doesn't know whether it is the sergeant's craven tactics, the primarch's stern gaze or the warning of a calamity that has already claimed millions of lives that drives him on: he just knows he has to end the Word Bearer. That the warrior's continued existence, without honour or true purpose, is an affront to the Emperor for whose service he was crafted. Aethon cannot bear the beating of the traitor's twisted hearts.

Striding through the bolt-storm, through the hololithic projection, Aethon grabs the sergeant by his plumed helm. He holds him there, the sizzling image of the primarch warping about them. Focusing his grief between the closing palms of his gauntlets, Aethon is oblivious to the Word Bearer's shrieks of panic and pain, and the boltgun blasting spasmodically in his enemy's tortured grip.

'What… have… you… done?' Aethon manages, his gauntlets seemingly having a despair and dark will of their own. The helm begins to crumple, along with the head inside. The captain's thumbs slip through the shattering eye-lenses. The Word Bearer lets out one last horrifying screech before dying in Aethon's hands.

Aethon releases him, allowing the traitor's corpse to crash to the ground. He stumbles back out of the hololithic projection, once more under the gaze of his primarch.

Aethon can hear the gunfire of battles beyond the command nexus. Across the vox he can hear Ultramarines dying, while Sergeant Urcus reports Word Bearers reinforcements arriving in the tunnels. The traitors will overrun their dwindling number. The command nexus, which they have fought so hard to secure, will fall again to the enemy.

Aethon looks up at Roboute Guilliman, and imagines himself before the primarch in the flesh. He cannot let that happen. He will not let that happen. He turns to survey the datastacks and cogitator banks, glowing red in their dormancy.

He has a command nexus. An operations centre he has fought hard to secure. He will use it.

'Brother Dactys, this is your captain,' Aethon orders across the vox. 'Withdraw to the teleportarium and secure the blast doors.'

'Captain?'

'Do as I command,' Aethon tells him before cycling through the channels. 'Brother Victurus, are you with me?'

'In a moment, my lord.'

Aethon moves through the nexus chamber, throwing levers, recalibrating runebanks and stabbing at buttons with chunky digits. Bit by bit, power is restored across the nexus chamber. Consoles and cogitators return to life. Lamps sizzle on before blinking to illumination across the vault and the tunnels beyond.

The stairwell shudders and groans as the Cataphractii Victurus climbs the tower, pausing in the doorway to aim a flurry of bolt-rounds out through the shattered window.

Aethon turns to consult a damaged screen that is somehow

still managing to display section schematics. 'Squad Urcus – fall back by columns to the command tower. Immediately,' he tells the Ultramarines fighting for their lives in the labyrinthine passageways.

'We've got Word Bearers flooding the tunnels,' Orestrian Urcus voxes back, *'in force and number.'*

'Is… Is Kurtha Sedd with them?'

'There's no way to tell. Do you wish us to abandon our hold points?'

'You won't be able to hold them for very long against such reinforcement,' Aethon tells him. 'And I will not sell your lives so cheaply, brothers. Fall back to the command tower. You will need to get to high ground. I intend to flood those tunnels with something else entirely.'

He can hear his friend barking orders. The vox-channel is open and enemy bolt-streams can be heard coming thick and fast as the Ultramarines engineer their retreat. The captain listens to the sergeant's grunts and exertions as he manhandles his Cataphractii suit around under the demands of a hurried tactical withdrawal.

Victurus scans the chamber, offering a sketched salute to the hololithic primarch in passing. 'Captain, we have enemy warriors approaching fast. Squad Rendrus will push through and hold position below.'

Aethon grunts, pausing to study the control system readouts one more time. 'No. We will bring them up here.'

'Steloc,' Urcus voxes uncertainly between hammering blasts of his own suppression fire. *'What are you doing?'*

'I'm going to purge the hypercoolant reservoir that cools the teleportarium reactors,' Aethon tells him, punching override commands into a nexus cogitator bank and setting warning klaxons howling. 'I'm going to flood the section. I've drawn the dogs in, and now I'm going to drown them.'

SIX

[mark: 72.39.39]

BROTHER LADON DIES. Like living traps, the tunnels gape
their darkness, waiting to snap shut with dagger-lined jaws.
The passageway lamps flicker and fizzle on. Everything sears
back to reality. Urcus's auto-senses reflexively cycle back to
regular spectra. The tunnel floor is red with enemy plate and
blood. Ladon is surrounded by Word Bearers. Like things of
darkness, the Urizen's spawn are revealed by the light in all
of their murderous glory. They stab at Ladon with their short
swords, their serrated combat blades and sacrificial knives,
working their weapons in through seals and between the
thick plates of his armour.

Maximon Scamander edges back in the bulk of his Cataphractii plate, spraying the passageway with bursts from his
combi-bolter. Word Bearers, brazen in their crimson armour,
are moving up the rocky corridor with wilful abandon, their
own weapons blazing back at the Ultramarines.

The sergeant tries to lead them out but Word Bearers appear from everywhere, the scripture of their plate glowing and their eye-lenses blazing green hatred. Urcus rounds a corner only to find the way blocked by wall-to-wall foes, recalled from some ambush point in the arcology complex. Heaving himself and his monstrous suit back around the corner, he feels the rock blasted away by the eager volley of shot sent his way. He can hear the stomp and step of enemy troops accelerating up the corridor at them, like hounds with a sudden scent.

'Scamander?' Urcus asks. He can hear the Ultramarine stifle his pain and frustration as bolt-round after bolt-round burrows into his sun-scorched suit.

'No,' the battle-brother manages.

He's not wrong. They are close to the command nexus, but trapped between Word Bearers intent on retaking the tower. 'I'm out,' Scamander warns his sergeant, the Ultramarine forced to put the last of his bolts into a wild Word Bearer throwing himself ahead of the pack. Scamander has the crackling hammer of his power fist waiting for the enemy. He puts him down, and then a second rushing in to take the fallen Word Bearer's place.

Urcus charges coruscating energies through the blades of his lightning claws and snorts within the sweaty confines of his helm. They are not going to make the tower. The sergeant makes a grim decision.

'Captain, this is Sergeant Urcus,' he voxes. 'We are inbound. You may purge the reservoir.'

'*Acknowledged*,' Aethon crackles back.

'Now, you treacherous curs,' Urcus growls. 'You want Calth? See if you can take it from us.'

Urcus hears the scrape of ceramite on rock. A Word Bearer is sidling up the wall to the corner. The sergeant doesn't wait. Stabbing a claw into the rock, Urcus tears away the corner with a furious crackle of energies and thuds the blades into the edging Word Bearer beyond. With a savage grunt, Urcus rips the traitor's arm, bolt pistol and all, from his armoured torso in a fountain of gore. Two Word Bearers follow, skidding around the corner before being splattered in their brother's blood. They are already firing their boltguns, the streams of fire fountaining sparks off Urcus's battered plate.

The sergeant lunges with his claws outstretched, the blades of both crackling gauntlets skewering the Word Bearers. Urcus runs them back into the tunnel wall, not giving the enemy time even to die before ripping his weapons free.

The passageway is full of enemies. Urcus slashes aside the furious blade of a chainsword, batting back the blur of monomolecular teeth before stabbing out with his other lightning claw. The force of a bloody and unexpected explosion knocks the sergeant forwards. The tunnel shakes. Dust cascades from the ceiling. Gore and shattered plate rain about Urcus as Brother Scamander is hit by a missile from a Word Bearers missile launcher. Urcus is down on his knees, the weight of his reinforced Cataphractii plate threatening to topple him over.

There are Word Bearers everywhere. The tunnel is choked with the treacherous fiends. Most are already gunning for the sergeant, while others stamp through the remains of his noble squad member.

Urcus's world becomes a maelstrom of violence and curses. Even within the protection offered by the Cataphractii suit, the experience takes his breath away. Mobbed by Word

Bearers and down on his knees, Urcus suffers an avalanche of blows. Fists fly and armoured boots stamp down furiously. His plate registers the savage impact of swords and chain weaponry, while at the same time feeling the wicked points of smaller sacrificial blades attempting to work their way through the layered plates of ceramite. Pistols discharge close to his helm, sending rounds thudding into the stone of the tunnel floor, while the deeper reports of boltguns can be heard as the weapons are manhandled into position amongst the swarm of armoured bodies. As several weapons crash into him at near point-blank range, Urcus roars. Even his monstrously reinforced plate cannot survive such a mauling for long.

A thunderous reverberation rolls up the passageway, a deep metallic *thunk* that passes through the maze of tunnels and the havoc unfolding within them. The Word Bearers do not seem to care; there isn't the slightest hesitation in the plate-buckling assault the mob of crazed legionaries is delivering. Urcus feels the sole of a stamping boot smash his helm to one side. A chainblade achieves momentary purchase, its teeth biting into the ceramite at the back of his leg and threatening to chew through it. An athame begins to prise his pack from the plate at his back, twisting its way through the seals. The mob is its own undoing, however. With so many Word Bearers wanting to claim the blood of an Ultramarines sergeant – an honoured Cataphractii, no less – each murderous attempt is a check, one upon another.

Inside the battered suit, Urcus finds his way to a kind of appreciation. Without the Word Bearers horde smashing him into the ground, the sergeant would almost certainly be already dead – blasted apart like poor Scamander.

Urcus knows what the booming announcement is, however. It is the sound of the Word Bearers' doom, as well as his own. His captain has fired the containment hatches and purged the hypercoolant reservoir. Any moment now the tunnel will be flooded with the cryogenic coolant used to ensure the operation of the teleportarium's reactors, freezing the Word Bearers in chemical fury.

Amongst the blast of boltguns, the kicks and the scrape of murderous daggers trying to find a way into the armoured coffin of his Cataphractii suit, the sergeant finds a moment of peace, of reflection.

You reap what you sow, Urcus admits to himself. *That's what I have always been taught. A neglected crop will canker in the same soil as a crop long cared for: like the Urizen's golden sons. An enemy unwatched for is the deadliest of foes.*

As a son of Calth or a Space Marine of the Emperor, I have failed. Upon my galactic watch and that of my Legion, enemies have butchered my brothers, razed a planet of the Imperium and slaughtered the people of my world. I am unworthy...

Urcus is tempted to let himself go, to become one with the violence visited upon his deserving body and Ultramarines plate. But it is not within him to surrender – not as a son of strongbacks toiling under the sun. Not as an Ultramarine, with the gifts to go on further than endurance allows or the mind can take.

No.

Never.

The sergeant wills himself to stand. To push not only his weary body up from the floor but also the weight of his monstrous suit and the mound of armoured foes in which he is buried. The skewering point of a power blade twisting between plates is nothing to him. The Word Bearer's fist slamming into the side of his crumpled helm is nothing to him. The dagger sawing at the seals of his throat is nothing to him.

Orestrian Urcus rises.

Word Bearers slide off his shattered suit. Some try to hold on, while others bring the gaping darkness of boltgun muzzles up to meet him. Urcus wills his lightning claws charged to furious intensity, spidery arcs of energy raining down to the bolt-cratered floor.

He forces the creaking Cataphractii suit around, throwing the Word Bearers clawing, stabbing and shooting into his back with it. One falls, knocked into a charging foe, while the remaining two soak up blasts from boltguns aimed at the spinning sergeant. As Word Bearers fall away and others in turn climb on to subdue him, Urcus heaves himself at the walls of the narrow tunnel. Charging his muscular frame and mauled plate into the rough rock, Urcus smashes Word Bearers into mangled corpses. The sergeant hammers himself at both enemy and wall with such force that he feels servos give, ceramite layers split and bones fracture.

He crushes a traitor sergeant's plumed helm between rock and pauldron. He caves in the faceplate of a Word Bearers Assault Marine with his armoured elbow. He rams his back brutally into the demolished tunnel corner, breaking the spine of an enemy warrior attempting to slit his throat.

Despite the decimation wrought on his foes, Urcus is still mobbed by throngs of crimson-plated maniacs. They are relentless. Boltguns crash at him. Chainswords threaten to cleave his helm in two.

Savagely shrugging the traitors off, Urcus pounds his way

back up the passageway. His heavy steps shake the walls and shower rock dust down onto the bloody ground. His target is one Word Bearer in particular, a battle-brother who is holding himself apart from the rest: the heavy weapons legionary who ended Maximon Scamander's existence.

Urcus charges at the Word Bearer. The legionary has a shot loaded, but not calibrated. He aims as best he can, launching the missile before the running Ultramarine can get too close.

Urcus crashes the bulk of his suit at the tunnel wall. The missile streaks away down the passageway, shredding the ceramite of the sergeant's pauldron before thundering into the Word Bearers mob behind. As it explodes, Urcus is blown across to the opposite wall.

Armoured carcasses and bits of bodies clatter messily to the floor after hitting the ceiling and walls. Word Bearers missing arms, faces and the will to live stumble through a miasma of bloody dust.

Urcus rescues himself from his own tumble and throws himself directly at the heavy weapons battle-brother. The Word Bearer still cannot quite believe what he has done. At first he tries to reload the launcher, but as Urcus's furious steps take him ever closer, the Space Marine abandons the heavy weapon and reaches for a bolt pistol. Two wild rounds is all Urcus gives him time for. Two rounds that spark harmlessly off the sergeant's redoubtable plate.

Urcus plunges his right-hand lightning claw into the Word Bearer's chest. The traitor grunts with agony and disbelief. Like a pugilist, Urcus pulls back with the right to bring in the left, tearing the crackling blades of the gauntlet out of the Word Bearer's punctured chest as he slams another set of skewering claws in. The traitor is all but dead as Urcus rips

the second claw out from his shattering chestplate. Bringing the right gauntlet back in, Urcus hammers the searing
blades of his lightning claw straight into the Word Bearer's
helm. With helm and skull split asunder, Urcus can see the
gory shock and surprise on his enemy's face. Withdrawing
the claw, he allows the butchered warrior to fall.

Urcus stands amongst the bodies of his fallen brothers. His
legionary brothers, blue of noble plate, and brothers crimson-
clad and fallen from their martial faith. The tunnel is thick
with death. It takes him a few moments before realising that
he shouldn't be able to breathe at all. The tunnel should be
submerged. The armoured corpses should be clattering along
with the current, frozen solid in the deluge of reservoir-
purged hypercoolant. The sergeant had heard the thunder
of the pneumatic locks clearly as his captain opened them
from the command nexus – and yet the only liquid that
Urcus was bathed in was the blood of his enemies.

'Urcus to Command,' he voxes.

'*Sergeant, you were issued a direct order to fall back to the command tower,*' Aethon says. Urcus can hear the concern behind
the reprimand. The vox-channel is suddenly drowned out in
the chatter of enemy gunfire. The tower is evidently under
siege.

'My column ran into a delay,' Urcus tells him.

'*What kind of delay?*'

'The indefinite kind,' Urcus says. He can hear the jangle
of plate echo up the corridor, followed by orders issued in
harsh Colchisian. 'There are going to be more if we don't
get those reservoir locks open.'

'*The nexus consoles report a problem with Lock Three,*' Aethon
says.

'It's probably jammed or corroded shut,' Urcus tells him. 'Leave it to me.'

'*Negative, sergeant,*' the captain orders. '*We will hold the enemy here.*'

'You are not seeing the reinforcements coming through here,' Urcus insists, watching the shadows of recalled Word Bearers lengthen on the corner of the tunnel walls.

'*We will hold as many for as long as required,*' Aethon says.

'You speak like a legionary of the Fourth, or the Seventh,' Urcus returns. 'That is not our way. It is not Guilliman's way. We uphold a tradition of victory. As a captain and an Ultramarine, you have to look to that and that alone. You owe as much to our people. To our world. Now, give the order. The order you know must be given if the sons of Guilliman are to see victory this day.'

Urcus waits. He waits as Word Bearers move through adjacent tunnels, blood-bent on finding Ultramarines and slaughtering them. He waits for his friend and commanding officer to order him to his death.

'*The order is given,*' Aethon says, his voice a leaden hiss against a background of storming gunfire. '*Sub-level five, section five. Fire the lock. Send our foe to the depths of a frozen hell.*'

'Affirmative, captain,' the sergeant says grimly. 'Urcus out.'

Urcus edges up to the corner. He can hear a good deal of movement – the thud of armoured boots and the priming of weapons. The Ultramarine's own claws crackle and spit by his sides. He waits until the stream of recalled Word Bearers moves on towards their officers and the command nexus.

The sergeant moves slowly. He has little choice; bodies litter the tunnel. The living move through adjacent passageways, all dread faith, presented weaponry and noisy plate.

Urcus's own Cataphractii Terminator suit is a ruin, a battered, sun-scorched wreck of battle-scarred ceramite and sparking cables. The suit of plate is a Legion relic in the making. Urcus had inherited it from his own sergeant, Ulyscon Perphidius. Perphidius had honoured the suit with many victories, and Urcus a fair few more. It is a belligerent thing: fearless and indomitable, like the battle-brother whose hulking form it protects.

Urcus attempts to move through the labyrinth of complex passageways without being noticed. This is impossible, however. Between the stone-cracking step, the protesting hydraulics and the sizzle and spark of cables and bundling, the Cataphractii suit is a walking advertisement of itself. Urcus thanks the primarch for the distant thunder of the siege. Without it the Word Bearers would hear him coming from a league away.

Word Bearers that do follow such indicators down side tunnels die quickly and economically. Urcus doesn't have the time or strength for extended engagements. He buries his lightning claws in bellies to tear out entrails or swipes heads from crackling shoulders. As enemies stomp past he grabs an inquisitive Word Bearer and holds him in an armoured lock, his arm crushing the foe's crimson helm and the head within.

Dropping the traitor, the sergeant powers on, up the crude-cut steps into Sub-Level 5 and through the maintenance holes bored out for the emergency purging of the hypercoolant reservoir. Below, Urcus can hear the boom of the reactors supplying unimaginable power to the bulk cargo teleportarium. His sensors register the drop in temperature. The barred gates his lightning claws tear aside advertise information and

warnings. They do not put the sergeant from his path. Neither do the first two sequential reservoir locks, both of which
lie open, their mighty purge doors pneumatically popped
from their round hatches. Everything glistens with a frosted
sheen. The sergeant's breath mists from his helm grille.

Stepping through, Urcus approaches the third lock. As he
feared, it is corroded: strangely coloured residue encrusts the
door as evidence of slow seepage. The sergeant's boots splash
through the sludge of long spoiled hypercoolant. He can hear
the pneumatic throb of the lock mechanism attempting to
obey instructions from the command nexus.

Urcus readies himself for the end. There is no time for final
thoughts or remembered words. Ultramarines are dying. He
charges the blades of his lightning claws.

'Freeze!' comes a voice. Urcus hears the sound of footfalls
in the tunnel between the locks. A pair of Word Bearers,
ghosting the sergeant since the auxiliary accessway. Foes he
had hoped would wait. Foes he had hoped to drown. The
sergeant allows himself a crooked smile. He can only imagine that they hold boltguns on his back. They wish to toy
with him. The traitors have a lone Ultramarine cornered. A
legionary apparently fleeing from the battle.

'Freeze?' Urcus mutters. 'You will. We all will.'

As he punches his claws into the corroded metal of the
hatch frame, Urcus hears the blast of boltguns behind him.
He tears at the lock with all of his might. Arcs of energy sizzle
across the surface of the metal. Urcus feels his own strength
and that of his powered suit combine with the pneumatic
insistence of the lock mechanism. At the same time, his
armour systems record the impact of enemy bolts ripping
into the layers of ceramite plate at his back. Urcus heaves,

and the lock gives. Clear hypercoolant sprays, foams and gushes from the opening. The liquid cascades over Urcus, steaming off the surface of his plate, setting off a series of alarms within his helm.

'What are you doing?' one Word Bearer manages, pausing in his fire to step back from the gush of hypercoolant spitting and spuming towards his boots.

'I'm winning,' Urcus tells him as he prises the reservoir lock open.

The sergeant is lost in a cascade of furious bubbles and escaping steam. Hypercoolant seethes over his plate, caking him in an instant frost. The Word Bearers turn to make their escape, but they are not nearly fast enough. A torrent of hypercoolant surges down the tunnel. The hatch has been blasted open, knocking Urcus back at the enemy, the flash-frozen bulk of his Cataphractii suit rolling and smashing through the Word Bearers at the head of the flood.

The legionaries stumble and flail their way awkwardly up the tunnel, driven on with the foaming surge of purged hypercoolant. Within his Terminator suit, Urcus wills mighty limbs to move. His helm display erupts with data and warnings, the Cataphractii suit alerting him to the dangers of splitting ceramite and frost-shattered plate.

Urcus knows he is asking a great deal of the armour. Before, both shell and spirit had stood against the stellar firestorm of Calth's surface. Here, in the dark bowels of the planet's interior, Urcus has plunged it into the caustic deep-freeze of coolant. The sergeant feels the phantom fingertips of icy death creep through the layers of ceramite and the suit's tortured workings. The cold begins to scald his already scorched skin. About him the sergeant hears the creak and contraction of the suit's superstructure and shrinking plates. Within his helm he sees tiny cracks blossom through his eye-lenses.

His body strikes the lip of a lock door, and the weight of the Cataphractii plate drags the Ultramarine down to the floor as coolant rages like a river past him. The Word Bearers are above, boltguns smashed from their grip, their limbs and plate tangled with the sergeant's own. He has killed them and they know it. It doesn't lessen their white-hot hatred or their fury, the heat of their ire the only thing keeping them alive in the monstrous freeze.

They hold onto the Ultramarine – or hold him down, Urcus can't tell which. With ceramite plates contracting and splitting across his Terminator suit, the sergeant tries to bring his lightning claws back to life. They have sizzled and shorted in the hypercoolant deluge. Urcus cares not. If he can only make his frozen limbs and ice-threaded hydraulics move he will drive the metal of his stabbing claws through his foes. He cannot, however, and lies rime-slick and prone beneath their murderous forms. One Word Bearer has a knife, a vicious sacrificial blade up which frost makes its glistening way. The second tries to draw a pistol from a holster but the weapon sticks, chilled to the inside of its armoured sheath.

Hypercoolant floods the tunnel, gushing and rising around them. Urcus watches through the clear liquid as the crimson of the Word Bearers' plate mists over white and the killers creak to a frozen halt. Soon they are all submerged, the entire tunnel one rushing, underground river.

Urcus feels his thick armour groan about him. The tactical display begins to flicker and fade. The reactor begins to die. Urcus feels cold to the core. His flesh burns against the plate. Meanwhile, his blood and his engineered form fight to keep any semblance of heat flowing through him.

Soon Urcus feels so numb that he can barely tell he is even there. Each breath is a throat-stripping gasp of blades. He closes his frost-encrusted eyes and allows the cold to take him. Everything is paralysis and pain. Everything is darkness. A frozen eternity passes. All Urcus can hear is the torrent of hypercoolant rushing about him from the purging reservoir.

Urcus hasn't felt this cold since Melior-Tertia. The Ultramarine remembers. It is all he has the power to do.

'What either the Priests of Mars or the xenos want with these iceballs, I'll never know,' Urcus tells his sergeant.

'The sum total of what you'll never know could be written in the Library of Ptolemy,' Sergeant Aethon tells him. 'And the Canticula Colchisium.'

Urcus grunts and stamps his cold feet and armoured boots into the frozen freightway. Ice rimes his Mark III power armour. The suit struggles to hold back the bitter factory-world cold. Snow storms about the Ultramarine and the White Spider, with only the flame-vomiting fusion towers and temple forges of Melior-Tertia visible through the gelid murk.

Urcus gets the impression of Legiones Astartes moving through the blizzard: warriors in blue and grey. Ultramarines and Word Bearers on the move. The greenskins are making a fresh assault on the Titan assembly yards of Velchius-Tannenberg. Urcus had heard as much over the vox.

'It is the nature of empire-building,' a voice intrudes across the channel. Urcus and Sergeant Aethon turn, to find Kurtha Sedd behind them. The Chaplain is a bleak phantom, his grim grey plate with its fluttering parchments seeming to coalesce from the

very snow as the storm dies down about them. 'Wasteland worlds like these would be of little consequence to anyone but for the fact they are claimed by someone else. The Empire of Mars wishes to expand its borders. An act of interstellar aggression. Now an alien empire wants them, for these worlds now come with the added incentive of smashing the ambitions of a rival race.'

'I don't know what that has to do with the warriors of Ultramar,' Urcus tells the Chaplain, readying his boltgun for the green harvest to come. The thought of the coming battle is keeping Urcus warm.

The White Spider and the Chaplain exchange a glance. Kurtha Sedd's green eye-lenses burn through the glacial haze. Urcus can almost hear the smiles shared by the Word Bearer and the sergeant.

'The Imperium is an empire within an empire,' Kurtha Sedd tells him.

Urcus primes his weapon. He turns to face the Chaplain.

'Well, I don't know about that,' Urcus tells him. 'I don't fight for the empires within. I fight for the Imperium of Mankind, with my father and for his. Our Lord Emperor's domain among the stars. The only empire of consequence. For the only empire that matters… is this one.'

Kurtha Sedd holds the Ultramarine's gaze. He draws his plasma pistol and unhooks his staff of office from his belt. The white storm picks up again about them. Using the crozius, the Chaplain indicates the way.

'Well said,' Kurtha Sedd tells him. 'Shall we?'

FOR A WHILE, Urcus thinks he is dead. The images flashing through his mind fade. The voices wither. The beating of his hearts becomes a background echo, lost and everlasting. Then, like waking from a dream, the waters recede. The hypercoolant drains about his prone form, evacuated from the reservoir and claimed by the depths. Above him, Urcus can see his two Word Bearers foes, their failed plate and the treacherous flesh within frozen solid. The sergeant can hear movement – armoured footsteps splashing through the shallows.

It hurts to even think. Everything is numb, like a body no longer there. The Cataphractii plate is an icy sarcophagus, its data feeds silent and spirit all but banished.

Urcus hears grit crunch under boot as closing figures tread about his ice-encrusted form, pivoting and turning. He blinks frost that speckles his cheeks. The sergeant can barely move his eyes, let alone his head or fast-frozen helm. The legionaries could be friends. They could be the traitors of the XVII Legion.

Urcus hears the crash of a boltgun. The ear-splitting thunder cuts through the chill ache of his thoughts. The Word Bearer above him shatters as the round smashes through him. Pieces of solid frozen plate and meat rain down about the Terminator sergeant. Another crash decimates the second, sending him to the floor in a cascade of crystalline shards.

A gilded blue helm drifts into view. It is Steloc Aethon. He steps about the frozen form of his friend, his combi-weapon drizzling smoke from where it put bolt-rounds through the two Word Bearers.

'Orestrian?' Aethon says. There is a kind of dread in the captain's voice.

Urcus cannot move. He lets his chest fall, allowing a painful breath to escape his lungs. Mist drifts from his faceplate grille. Aethon nods to himself as much to Urcus. 'Bring cables!' the captain commands. 'We shall boost-start his pack using my own. Hold on, sergeant.'

As his breath drizzles away, Urcus manages to send a word or two with it. Aethon gets down on his knees, putting the side of his helm to the sergeant's vox-grille.

'The only empire...' Urcus tells him, each syllable a half-remembered agony, '...is this one.'

The captain pushes himself back up, his hulking suit like a small mountain looming over Urcus. He looks down at the sergeant, lost in thought.

'One empire,' Aethon repeats. 'One Imperium.' He nods, before looking down at the crater in his plate, still sparking in his side. A decision is reached. Clearly a painful one. Aethon changes vox-channel. 'Brother Nereon, this is the captain: status.'

'*The coolant is receding, captain,*' Nereon reports. '*The command nexus is ours. The enemy is either dead or fled.*'

'Excellent,' Aethon tells him. 'We have your sergeant.'

'*Thank the primarch,*' Urcus hears Nereon say.

'Hold the command nexus,' Aethon orders. 'Our victory here has been bought dearly. I want you to bring the tower vox-station online.'

'*Yes, captain.*'

'Broad spectrum communication to all Ultramarines under my command.'

'*Ready. Confirm message to be transmitted?*'

'Communication as follows,' Aethon says. 'Guilliman's order temporarily rescinded. I want Kurtha Sedd.'

'*Captain?*'

'You heard me, brother,' Aethon tells him, looking down at Urcus. The sergeant stares back. 'Captain's orders – bring me the Chaplain alive.'

SEVEN

[mark: 132.20.02]

As the plant its roots or the hab its foundations, the body legionary requires a base – no matter how temporary.

So the primarch teaches, Aethon reminds himself. The tunnel echoes with the captain's purposeful footsteps. He passes Brother Endymias on sentry duty. The Space Marine stands to attention at his post and offers the officer a salute.

Brothers of the XIII do not revel in fortification as art. Neither are they at the mercy of the wind, mobile, flexible and free. For the Ultramarine favours all paths, to the exclusion of none. Strategic circumspection is his shield, upon which the enemy batters itself. Tactical conviction, his blade – worked through the best efforts of the foe. Ready to deliver victory with a thoughtful, killing blow. Like the vessels of the void, powerful and proud, the Ultramarine makes way when required, runs down upon his opponent as opportunity provides and assumes defensive station when tactically prudent to do so.

For Aethon of the 19th, at war with his fallen brothers and the darkness, it has become tactically prudent to assume such a station. He weaves through the gauntlets, temporary cover assembled from superfluous machinery and supplies. Barricades laced to offer hold points for scrambled Ultramarines and created to slow the advance of an attacking enemy force.

The passageway bottlenecks and choke points are only the beginning. Before the hypercoolant had drained away and the frozen bodies of Word Bearers were shattered under bolt and boot, Aethon had ordered preparations to secure the command nexus as a permanent base of operations. Ultramarines under the captain's command were recalled and reassigned. Supplies were brought in from the teleportarium depot and communication lines secured, while the coolant reservoirs were duly replenished.

Being a sub-level operations post initially created to aid in the construction of the surrounding subterranean networks, it boasted no medicae centre. It is for this reason, and the fact that many injured Ultramarines and civilians cannot be moved, that Aethon has retained a camp up in the outer complexes.

Patrols have been organised, sentry posts established, tunnels barricaded or collapsed to reduce the number of ways into the command nexus. Within a relatively short space of time, Aethon and his Space Marines have turned a basic subterranean outpost into a defensible command centre for Ultramarines operations in the area.

Neighbouring arcologies, storage facilities and complexes have been explored and cleared of enemy contingents. Orbital vox and complex communication systems are re-established. The Word Bearers have been driven back to the

depths – into shadow, where they belong. The Ultramarines establishment about the command nexus has been
unmolested and the silence from the enemy so deafening
that Aethon has been tempted to regard it as a kind of victory. Guilliman warns, however, against such complacence.
Only the primarch has the wisdom to prepare his sons for
the benighted path ahead, and even he has stumbled. Even
Guilliman, with his faultless codification and martial vigi-
lance, had been blind to the betrayal that has swallowed his
Legion whole.

Aethon thinks of his Word Bearers foes. He has killed scores
of traitors but once more he finds himself musing on Kurtha
Sedd. For Aethon, the lines of the Chaplain's face had once
denoted a quiet intelligence – a solemn wisdom. Now, as he
remembers his former friend and ally, he sees only the hau-
teur of his thin lips, the hate and distrust of too-keen eyes.

What kind of victory would Kurtha Sedd grant him, the
captain wonders? Surrender is unlikely. The Word Bearers are
traitors but they are still Legiones Astartes. Like the Ultramarines, they have been gene-bred to fight and through
psycho-indoctrination, conditioned to win. It is not within
them to submit to an enemy force. No, Kurtha Sedd would
make the captain kill him. The Word Bearers have chosen a
doomed path, but unlike other Legions long lost, they have
chosen their destroyers. This time it is the Ultramarines' turn
to bear witness, to judge and to execute their gene-kin.

As Aethon approaches the teleportarium, he entertains one
further possibility. Something unthinkable, given the horrors
of days gone by, yet a notion irresistible in its dark appeal.
Regardless of his past service to the Emperor and mankind,
Kurtha Sedd deserves to die. Aethon owes the Chaplain a

debt of blood, however – an obligation he will now probably never get to fulfil. Despite the foul actions of the XVII
Legion, the honourable debt burns in Aethon's chest.

The Word Bearers have changed beyond recognition, cor-
rupt of purpose and hate-filled of heart. The Ultramarines
have not changed: their honour is intact, and will remain
so as long as they remember who they are.

For Aethon that means honouring his debts. He knows he
cannot speak against his primarch's orders, but perhaps – just
perhaps – he might be able to offer Kurtha Sedd something
in return. A death for a life. An honourable death. Perhaps
he can give the Word Bearers Chaplain the chance to atone
for his betrayal. A choice. The opportunity to acknowledge
his unworthiness in the eyes of the Emperor and meet his
end in his own way. A warrior's death.

If he can just speak to Kurtha Sedd, without the fury of gunfire and the treachery of Lorgar's dark intention. If he could
speak to Kurtha Sedd as once they had, Aethon thinks he
might be able to convince the Chaplain. Convince him to
answer the call in his heart, to appease the agony of dishon-
our with sacrifice. To save the lives of countless Ultramarines
with the taking of his own. Perhaps the wise Chaplain could
convince other brothers to follow his example. Between
them, they might repair a little of the horrific damage done
to both Legions in this, the most doomed chapter in their
history.

Aethon looks down at his cratered side, the searing injury
delivered by the Word Bearers Chaplain on the battlefield
above. Had that been Kurtha Sedd? The captain knows in his
aching bones that it had, though the odds against it are phe-
nomenal. It could never be easy to convince such a proud

warrior to turn his death-dealing weaponry on himself, but Aethon has come to the dread conclusion that he has to try.

'Aethon to Command,' he says, adjusting his vox-channel and rounding the corner to the teleportarium.

'Acknowledged, captain,' Brother Medon returns from his post up in the command tower. *'Proceed.'*

'Have Sergeant Dardanus bring the prisoners up to the chamber below the command tower,' Aethon says. He has placed what remains of Squad Sephirus in charge of the small number of traitors the Ultramarines have managed to take. Most Word Bearers are hell-bent on killing their foe and themselves in the process, but Dardanus and his men had managed to capture some traitors alive. 'Status report,' Aethon continues.

'Squad Valin have returned from their sweep of the Thesprotia sub-arcology. Enemy contingents have fallen back into the skein of lower-level passageways there. Sergeant Valin seeks permission to pursue.'

'Denied,' Aethon tells him. 'Sergeant Valin will complete his sweep and consolidate. He will not be drawn into an ambush.'

'Acknowledged, captain,' Brother Medon says. He is used to relaying the bluntness of Aethon's orders.

'Losses?'

'Brother Serapho,' Medon informs him. *'A collapse in the Conduis Seculorum. His acting sergeant suspects the enemy but no contingents reported. Xantius Dolomon and Cydor Rhadamanth are reported as injured. I've sent them back to the outer complexes.'*

'Go on.'

'Squad Tynon reports that it has the traitor Maldreq Fal cornered in the Vault-Vexillium,' Medon crackles across the vox. *'They request reinforcements to finish the Word Bearers there.'*

'Tell Sergeant Tynon that I have already reinforced the Vault-Vexillium with his Terminators. Further battle-brothers cannot be spared.'

Aethon's Ultramarines are beset on all sides by marauding contingents of Word Bearers. The traitors are finding one another in the darkness, gravitating towards officers and feverish Chaplains before turning their emboldened number on their similarly trapped foe.

The madman known as Shan Varek has been routinely hitting their positions with guerrilla actions from the south. Maldreq Fal and his fanatics, meanwhile, are like a tick buried in the expanding territory Aethon's Ultramarines have systematically cleared, refusing to give up their hold. Kurtha Sedd's dread warriors, who entered the arcology networks at the same time as Aethon's own men, have been washed back into the depths by the purged hypercoolant reservoir.

'I have Brother Tithonon for you, captain,' Medon says, *'patched through from the* Aeternian. *He wishes to know if his battle-brothers have arrived safely.'*

'Stand by,' Aethon tells the command tower as he reaches the teleportarium blast doors. Using the command tower's vox-station and hardware connected to a surface booster array, Aethon's men have made contact with the *Aeternian*, an Ultramarines vessel stranded in orbit. A victim of the Word Bearers' initial attack, the *Aeternian* and its transports were critically damaged and could not escape the stellar storm along with the rest of the withdrawing XIII Legion fleet.

Just managing to hold station behind ravaged Calth and out of the poisoned star's blaze of deadly radiation, Brother Tithonon returned the command tower's communication. Eager to get down to the surface and join the fight against the fell Word Bearers, Tithonon and Brother Pronax of Aethon's cohort were attempting to integrate the homing signals of the *Aeternian*'s failing teleporters with the bulk cargo teleportarium.

Aethon finds an Ultramarines sentry in power armour and Brother Pronax waiting at the door. Pronax puts up a gauntlet as his captain approaches.

'Captain…'

He doesn't need to say any more.

'Open it,' Aethon orders.

The sentry complies and the teleportarium door rumbles upwards. Gore dribbles down from the inside of the door in sticky rivulets, falling with the upward movement. The teleportarium is cast in a red haze. Aethon takes several steps forwards. The chamber is a scene of utter carnage that no hand-held weapon could ever hope to create. Struggling with the faltering link between them, the bulk industrial teleporter and the high-grade teleportarium of the Ultramarines warship have shredded their subjects. The unimaginably powerful forces at work have embedded pieces of cobalt-blue shrapnel in the walls and floor, while dousing the receiving chamber in a fine spray of blood and tiny scraps of flesh.

Aethon stands there. Six warriors have perished, although for absence of anything that might be described as even a single body, his eyes alone could not have told him as much. The captain breathes deeply and takes it all in. Takes responsibility. Takes these fresh deaths upon his shoulders like all the others.

'Medon,' he voxes, his voice hollow. 'Tell Brother Tithonon that his brothers were… unsuccessful in their translation. Tell him to hold his position, that the systems are not trustworthy and that we are therefore unable to receive him and his brothers at this time.'

'*Captain*,' Medon says, his enthusiasm out of place with the macabre scene in which Aethon stands. '*I'm getting a new transmission.*'

'From orbit?' Aethon asks.

'*From another nexus*,' Medon tells him. '*From another sub-level vox-station.*'

'Name and location,' Aethon orders, turning away from the aethyric slaughter of the teleportarium.

'*Brother Pelion*,' Medon informs the captain, '*fighting under Tetrarch Nicodemus. Location, Arcology Magnesi.*'

The captain nods to himself. Tauro Nicodemus lives – the primarch's champion and Tetrarch of Saramanth. Aethon knew Nicodemus had been fighting at Lanshear. He must have entered the arcology network with his men at a surface entrance further along the system.

'Return location and my designations,' Aethon says, stepping away from the teleportarium. 'Ask him for his. I want to be sure we are talking to Ultramarines. I'm on my way.'

He turns once more to take in the horror of the chamber: to face Pronax and the sentry. There are no words.

'We'll take care of it, captain,' says Brother Pronax.

Aethon nods his thanks and hurries away. The captain hates himself for abandoning the scene to his subordinates but the opportunity to join forces with another Ultramarines contingent and defer command to a superior officer cannot be ignored.

By the time he gets to the command nexus Aethon finds the shape of Orestrian Urcus there, looming over Brother Medon in his ruined Cataphractii plate.

'The signal's gone,' Urcus tells him, the decimated shell of his armour creaking and scraping as he moves.

'Get them back,' Aethon orders.

'I can't,' Brother Medon says. 'The transmission was cut off either at the source or somewhere between Arcology Magnesi and here.'

'Sabotage?' Aethon asks.

'Word Bearers could have damaged the hardware at any point between us,' Medon agrees. 'It wouldn't be difficult.'

'But almost impossible to isolate where and repair the severed cabling,' Sergeant Urcus says. 'The enemy want us isolated.'

'Thank you, sergeant,' Aethon says absently. 'It was Nicodemus?'

'One of his men,' Urcus says. 'Hylas Pelion.'

'I transmitted our location,' Brother Medon says, 'but I don't know if they got it.'

'Hopefully they won't need it,' the captain says, adjusting the dials and switches on a nearby runebank. 'We have theirs.'

Basic schematics flash up on the screen. 'Magnesi. Magnesi,' Aethon says to himself. 'There.' He taps the screen with a ceramite fingertip.

'It's close,' Medon says with obvious approval.

'No,' Urcus corrects him. Unlike Aethon and the sergeant, Imbrius Medon does not hail from Calth. 'It belongs to a distinct subterranean system.'

'He's right,' Aethon confirms unhappily.

'But I thought all the systems were connected?' Medon says.

'They are,' the captain admits. 'But we aren't going to find a route on an arterial schematic like this.'

'We'll have to go deeper,' Urcus suggests. 'Through the undervaults, sub-levels and natural formations.'

Aethon agrees. He adds grimly, 'Down into the darkness, where the Word Bearers wait for us.'

'I'll go,' Urcus tells him. 'My squad will punch a way through and rendezvous with the Tetrarch and this Pelion at Arcology Magnesi.'

'No,' the captain says. As the two Terminators debate the issue, Medon turns aside to receive reports from Ultramarines contingents under Aethon's command.

'What is it?' the captain demands.

'Sergeant Tynon is dead, captain,' Medon tells him.

'The traitors?' Urcus asks.

'Maldreq Fal has escaped again,' Medon says. 'Squad Tynon is pulling out of the Vault-Vexillium.'

'Have them hold the vault entrance,' Aethon commands. 'I'll go down there myself if I have to.'

'You might have to,' Medon admits. 'I have no available units.'

'Ulantus Remulo?' Aethon had charged Remulo's squad with a floating brief, making them responsible for plugging gaps opening up in the arcology defence.

'Has a confirmed sighting of Shan Varek in the Didelphii Underwarrens,' Medon tells his captain. 'You cleared his squad to engage enemy forces if they saw an opportunity.'

'Who has Tynon's squad?' Aethon asks, his optics darting across the runescreen's crude schematic. His Ultramarines are stretched, caught between the demands of securing the complex from enemy attack and the necessities of expanding their territory to deny the enemy a foothold.

'Deucalius Chalcodon.'

'Tell Chalcodon to hold that vault,' Aethon says. 'His captain commands it. Pull Dromedon Pax and his squad back from the outer complexes.'

'Squad Pax have been out of contact for almost twelve hours,' Medon informs him.

'Damn it,' Aethon says. 'Keep trying to raise them and if you do, tell them to fall back to support Squad Tynon at the Vault-Vexillium.'

'Yes, brother-captain.'

'Maldreq Fal and Shan Varek are accounted for,' Aethon says. 'What of Kurtha Sedd?'

'I have no confirmations of that target, captain,' Brother Medon admits.

'He's here…'

'No encounters with the Word Bearers retreating into the sub-levels,' Medon tells Aethon. 'Some stragglers fired upon in the western ductways, but I don't think they are part of that contingent.'

'With respect, captain,' Urcus says, his Cataphractii suit rattling like scrap about him, 'we need to make contact with Tetrarch Nicodemus and his men. With extra legionaries we could eradicate the enemy threat and truly consolidate our position.'

'Agreed,' Aethon tells him.

'Then I am cleared to reassume my duties?'

'Look at yourself,' Aethon says. The sergeant is a shadow of the legionary he had once been. His plate is a creaking wreck of battle-bleached ruin, barely responding to its hydraulics and servos. Three of his lightning-claw blades have been frost-shattered to half-talons, while the sergeant's helm is a smashed remnant consisting of little more than an ugly faceplate grille covering his mouth.

'My plate still has service to offer,' Urcus insists, 'and my weapons stand ready.'

Aethon stands in thought.

'Walk with me,' he says, leaving the command nexus. In his rattling plate, Sergeant Urcus follows.

'I'm sending you to the outer complexes,' Aethon says as they exit the tower and make their way to a side chamber beyond.

'My injuries are superficial, captain,' Urcus tells him.

'I know,' Aethon says. 'Dromedon Pax's original instructions were to check in with the injured and civilians camped in the outer complexes, but we have not been able to raise the camp or Pax's squad for twelve hours. It's probably a communications difficulty as a result of stellar storm interference but I want to make sure. You are to take your squad and report back what you find.'

'What of the Tetrarch?' Urcus asks as they pass Ultramarines sentries and enter the cavernous chamber. Aethon grunts. He has given Urcus a duty. It simply isn't the one that the sergeant desires.

The captain looks up to see warriors, both Ultramarines and Word Bearers prisoners, in the chamber. Aethon counts four sons of Lorgar, strung in chains that descend from the cavern ceiling.

'I have my man for that,' Aethon says as Acting Sergeant Dardanus turns with the remains of Squad Sephirus. Dardanus offers a salute to the captain as he crosses the cavern.' Squad Sephirus will traverse the depths,' Aethon tells Urcus, 'and make contact with Tauro Nicodemus, returning with the Tetrarch's orders. Sergeant Dardanus is about to be relieved of his present duty.'

'Brother, is this wise?' Urcus urges.

'You said it yourself,' Aethon tells the sergeant. 'The only empire is this one. I will not stand idly by and watch the Legiones Astartes carve up the Imperium for their own dark desires. Not while we can still do something about it.'

'We can,' Urcus insists. 'We can face down treachery with bolt and blade. We can wipe the galaxy clean of any evidence that the Word Bearers ever existed.'

'As has been done with Legions before?'

'Aye,' Urcus says, 'and will be done again, if needs be.'

'Do you hear that, sergeant?' Aethon asks.

'Hear what?'

'The sound of history repeating itself, in our words and deeds,' Aethon says.

'Kurtha Sedd...'

'...is a traitor to the Imperium, to his genic inheritance and his Emperor,' Aethon seethes. 'He will die for what he has done – but if there is a chance that by reaching out to him we can turn the course of these grave events even in the least part, then I am willing to try. I know Kurtha Sedd–'

'No one truly knows these trustless dogs,' Urcus says as they approach Dardanus. Brothers Tibor and Aloysio have their boltguns pointed at the Word Bearers.

'Sergeant,' Dardanus says, acknowledging Urcus coolly.

'Acting sergeant,' Urcus hisses back through his grille, laying a hint of emphasis on the word *acting*.

Urcus slows, allowing Aethon to approach the prisoners with Dardanus.

'The prisoners,' Dardanus announces. 'As you requested, captain.'

Aethon walks up to the chained Word Bearers. He looks down on the wretched Space Marines. Their plate is smashed and awash with blood from injuries sustained in the course of their capture. One has lost his helm; his head is shaven and his features sharp. They stare at Aethon with dark intelligent eyes and burning green lenses. Something about the chains bothers the captain. With so little honour to be earned in the underworld and its desperate engagements, the shackles seem unnecessary. The trappings of torture.

'What do you think you're doing?' Aethon says. He is angry. At his men. At himself.

'Taking prisoners,' Dardanus repeats, a little unsure of himself. 'These were the only survivors.'

'Taking prisoners, to what end?' Aethon says, casting a furious gaze across the miserable Word Bearers. He gestures at the chains binding their wrists and ankles. 'What were you going to do? Ask them why they betrayed us and the Imperium? Get them to beg for forgiveness?'

Dardanus is silent. He understands he is being asked a rhetorical question. He casts a look at Urcus but the sergeant shakes his head.

The captain moves with sudden fury, prompting the Word Bearers to rattle in their chains and the gauntlets of the Ultramarines to creak about their boltguns. Aethon draws a bolt pistol from his belt and holds the muzzle before the helm of one of the Word Bearers.

'What will we learn from them? Nothing. Will they speak? Of course not,' Aethon says, his eyes burning with righteous hatred. 'And that's assuming they know anything. I'd be surprised if they even know the locations of their other units. Isn't that right, traitor?'

The prisoner keeps the captain waiting. When he speaks every word is rasping with spite.

'What I know is beyond your understanding. What

Kurtha Sedd will visit upon you will be beyond your comprehension.'

Aethon takes a step back. He stares at the prisoner, losing himself for a moment in the blood-slick crimson of his plate.

'Kurtha Sedd,' Aethon repeats back. 'You belong to the same company as Kurtha Sedd?'

'I do.'

Aethon's mind is a maelstrom of dark thoughts. Half-comprehended plans become a searing reality in his mind. He mutters a curse and repeats the Chaplain's name. The bolt pistol comes down at his side. Aethon feels the eyes of both Word Bearers and Ultramarines on him as he walks back and forth to the cavern wall. He buries his armoured fist in the wall, creating a crater in the stone. It is time to commit. Commit to a plan. Commit to a possibility. Commit the lives of his men to a gamble – a bet that Kurtha Sedd still has some scintilla of nobility residing in his afflicted heart.

'Take them down,' he says finally.

'Brother-captain?'

'I said take them down. Unchain them.'

He approaches the prisoner who had spoken once more, staring into the deep green of the legionary's eye-lenses, attempting to get a measure of the Space Marine beyond.

'I once owed a great debt to Kurtha Sedd,' Aethon says, to both the Word Bearers and his own men. 'What happened on Calth these last days has cancelled it. But...' He breaks off. 'But I believe in honour, even if the Seventeenth Legion has abandoned all notion of it. You will return to Kurtha Sedd. Tell him you carry a message from Steloc Aethon. Tell him he has a choice. Tell him if he and the men under his command surrender, they will be granted a swift, honourable execution. That is far more than any of you deserve, but I will do this in memory of the brotherhood we once shared.'

'Captain…' Urcus says.

Aethon turns to regard his friend and sergeant. He walks away from the prisoners.

'What?' Aethon says.

'Are you serious?'

'I am.' He shoots a glance back at Dardanus and his squad. 'Do as I said,' he tells them.

'Honour does not require you to do this,' Urcus says, keeping his voice low.

'Perhaps not. But the decision is mine.'

'It is a decision that affects all of us.'

'And what will be the consequences of sending these four wretches back to Kurtha Sedd?' Aethon hisses. 'What vital information about us do they possess? How will they shift the balance of power? How will they harm our position?'

'They are four warriors we will have to fight again,' Urcus tells him, the logic harsh in his words.

'A risk we can take.'

'But why take it?' one of Dardanus's squad asks of his captain. 'I don't understand.'

Urcus and Dardanus both go to silence the legionary, but Aethon brings his gauntlet up. His battle-brothers deserve an explanation, when Aethon will be putting them in harm's way. Kurtha Sedd's way.

'It may be more than he would offer me now, but I will give Kurtha Sedd this chance. There is too much in our past for me to ignore, Envixus. If he will choose this way to end the war, I will let him. I hope he will.'

'You can't *believe* he will,' Envixus protests.

'I don't know,' Aethon answers with hollow honesty. The cavern falls silent, until suddenly it booms with the captain's words. 'Whatever fate he chooses, I want Kurtha Sedd to know I am here.' He points at the Word Bearers. To the Word Bearer who had spoken the Chaplain's name. 'Speak *my* name. If you do nothing else in your miserable existence, do this thing. Tell him I am here. Tell him I am looking for him.' To Envixus he says, 'He won't be able to ignore me any more than I can him. We will draw him out.'

Brother Envixus shakes his head as Aethon turns to leave. 'Theoretical – these are personal decisions, not tactical ones.'

'Practical – the enemy will be forced to respond,' Aethon counters, indicating that Sergeants Urcus and Dardanus should follow him. 'The initiative is ours. Now send them on their way.'

Dardanus gives Brother Envixus, the newest addition to his squad, a furious glare before indicating that he should join Squad Sephirus in unchaining the Word Bearers.

Aethon and Sergeant Urcus wait for Dardanus outside the entrance of the side cavern. The captain stares at an arcology map carved into the rocky wall.

'Acting sergeant.'

'Brother-captain?'

'I have a further duty for you and your squad,' Aethon tells him.

'Name it, captain.'

Aethon indicates a position on the basic map with an armoured finger.

'This is us,' he says. 'This, here, is the Arcology Magnesi. Earlier, Brother Medon received a vox-tranmission from Tetrarch Nicodemus and his Ultramarines running operations out of

that system. As you can see, there is no direct route from
here through the underworld network to Magnesi shown
at this level. We believe that one might lie deeper down in
the sub-levels.'

'You want me to make contact with the Tetrarch?'

'Yes,' Aethon agrees. 'We must pool our resources if we
are to survive the Word Bearers in this section, and we lost
contact with the Tetrarch shortly after that communication.'

'Sabotage?' Dardanus asks.

'Most likely,' Urcus says.

'Forgive me, brother-captain,' Dardanus says, seemingly
unable to let go of what had just happened in the chamber
beyond. 'What of the prisoners?'

'You will take them with you and cut them loose on the
lower levels,' Aethon orders.

'You should hold on to them for as long as feasible,' Sergeant Urcus says. 'Kurtha Sedd and his men retreated through
those levels and into the depths. If you run into trouble you
can always use the prisoners as collateral to be exchanged
for free passage.'

Aethon nods in agreement.

Dardanus looks from Urcus to his captain. He nods slowly.

'I'll ready my squad and my prisoners, captain.'

'Very good, sergeant,' Aethon tells him with a weak smile.
He watches Dardanus return to his men.

When the acting sergeant is out of earshot, Urcus asks: 'Permission to speak candidly?'

'Proceed,' Aethon says.

'He's going to cut loose those Word Bearers in enemy territory,' Urcus says, nodding at the departing Dardanus. 'And
possibly have his throat cut for his efforts.'

'Possibly,' Aethon agrees gravely.

'And then have those traitors glaring back at us over a boltgun.'

'What's your point?' Aethon says. The two Ultramarines stare at one another through the murk of the command nexus, before breaking into the grim smiles of Space Marines courting their doom.

'Still,' Urcus says, moving noisily across the chamber, 'before I go, candidly: I wouldn't waste this plan on a feral-world dog.'

'Understood,' Aethon tells him. 'Would you like your opinion noted in the mission log?'

Urcus leaves to gather his own squad. Over his shoulder the sergeant calls, 'That would make me a feral-world dog.'

EIGHT

[mark: 134.09.33]

ORESTRIAN URCUS SEES the bodies first. There are innocents everywhere, citizens of Calth who had taken refuge in the arcology complex just as the Ultramarines had, and as the Word Bearers had. Their corpses lie broken and twisted on the complex floor, the vaulting spatters and pools of gore about them like a remembrancer's nightmare daubed on canvas. People have been blasted apart with bolt-rounds and torn to ragged shreds by chainblades. Some have had their throats slit, while others have simply been brained and broken by the butts of boltguns and armoured fists.

As Squad Urcus and their sergeant take in the slaughter, they see evidence of citizens gunned down in their cots whilst trying to escape or hide. Some of the corpses have been mutilated with symbols carved into their flesh, while others evince the bloody mess of uneven combat. It is a demonstration of what happens when a genetically engineered warrior of the Emperor – powerful and armoured – visits his wrath upon the forms of mere humans.

'This is abominable,' Brother Eurotas growls across the vox.

'Those monsters...' Pontus adds.

'Let's finish our sweep,' Urcus tells them, but the sergeant is no less disturbed by the bloody scene. While Kurtha Sedd's Word Bearers have seemingly retreated into the shadows, others have been sent back to the outer complexes to hit the vulnerable and the wounded. This is the reality of fighting an underworld war, cavern by cavern, at such close quarters, Urcus reasons, trying to bring some kind of sense to the slaughter.

Pushing on into the arcology system, the Ultramarines had protected the rag-tag collections of terrified citizenry from the horror of front-line battle. In doing so, even with sentries and a defensible position, they had left the camp vulnerable to attack, the Word Bearers having sworn to make the Ultramarines suffer in whatever depraved fashion they could. An attack in retaliation for losing the command nexus.

The sergeant tries to find comfort in his primarch's teachings.

In every victory resides a future defeat; in every survivor, the potential for death anew. For like the galaxy, war is an endless spiral of violence visited and visited upon. All are part of such a spiralling descent into carnage and some are even engineered for it. Fight not its irresistible pull. Fight on into inevitability. For a galactic singularity awaits us there. The unification of mankind, as the Emperor intends it – where humanity reigns supreme among the stars, as one and finally free from the myriad threat of its enemies.

Urcus trudges through the butchery, his armoured footfalls

spreading gore and sending bolt-casings clinking across the
floor. He considers whether the Emperor had had such slaughter in mind. Had he seen in his son Lorgar such a threat? Had
he considered the possibility that a day would come when
one of his own Legions might be one of those myriad threats?

'Be ready,' Urcus tells his much-reduced squad of Cataphractii Terminators across the vox. 'Our foe might still be here.'

The Ultramarines move warily through the outer complex,
making the best use of cover they can. The primer of Brother
Pontus's heavy flamer hisses in the background, while the
sergeant's claws crackle from the front.

The blasted bodies of fleeing citizens give way to acrid decimation of the camp. It looks as if the Word Bearers have
used a flamer on the camp infirmary, bathing the unconscious, the wounded and the dying in fire. The citizens of
Calth, looking for aid and protection in the arcology, have
found only the horror of death here. Urcus casts a grim gaze
over charred bodies huddled together in fear, scorched into
one mass of smouldering flesh.

There also, the Ultramarines find their brothers. The grievously injured and battle-inoperative. Sons of Guilliman who
had been sent back to the camp to heal, while watching over
the growing crowds of terrified citizens. A number have been
roasted within their battle-smashed plate. Others – limping, crawling, peering through crusted blood and bandages
– have clearly mounted a determined defence. Such brave
warriors now lie mauled on the floor and stripped of their
weaponry. Urcus steps over a battle-brother who still has a
pair of sacrificial daggers in his chest, then an Ultramarine
so riddled with shot and shell that he is merely a mound of
mulched flesh and shattered plate on the ground.

Further up the chamber, as the squad weaves its way through pillars and piles of corpses, Urcus sees a blinding flash. Dimming and flashing, dimming and flashing. The sergeant approaches with his Terminators trudging cautiously behind. Ahead Urcus makes out a large inner blast door, its cratered control panel sparking from a stray bolt-round. The malfunctioning door mechanism hauls the heavy blast door up off the floor with a hydraulic *thunk* before allowing it to crash back down.

With each failed attempt to open, the toxic brilliance of the stellar storm outside reaches inside. Reasoning that the outer blast door must have failed in some way, Urcus slows. The blinding blaze of intruding brilliance reaches in, momentarily turning everything to searing whiteness before fading suddenly with the dropping of the blast door.

'Hold,' the sergeant says. He is beginning to rethink the charred bodies in the camp. 'Auspectrals?'

'Compromised,' Brother Nereon tells him. 'The section is flooded with radiation. We shouldn't linger, sergeant.'

'Have faith in your plate, brother,' Urcus tells him, rattling in the smashed remains of his own, 'and it will protect you. Comms?'

'Beyond suit to suit?' Victurus says. 'Not functional.'

Urcus nods. He can hear the hiss and snap of his own vox as the thudding door bleaches the slaughter chamber with the poisoned light of the Veridian star.

'Pontus, Nereon,' Urcus commands. 'Check those side vestibules.'

'Aye, sergeant,' the pair return, peeling off with weapons held high.

The blast door rises, and eye-scalding brilliance floods the chamber, hitting the Ultramarines Cataphractii suits like a physical force and causing Urcus to squint against the glare. As the door rises, Urcus thinks he sees something – the outline of something big. He sniffs at the blistering air through his grille. Magna-coil unguent. Barrel smoke. The old tang of internment fluid and leakage.

The sergeant's hearts thud in his chest.

'A Dreadnought!'

As he calls out to his squad, Urcus sees the outline of the monstrous machine, a faint silhouette eclipsed by the raging light. Contemptor-pattern. Huge. Armoured. Urcus notes the colossal power fist hanging by its side and the assault cannon fixed in position to fire. Urcus heaves himself to the right, his shattered suit responding sluggishly. Moving behind a pillar, Urcus reaches out for Phalon Victurus, but the Ultramarine is already dead. Plucked from his sergeant's grasp, the Terminator is torn backwards before a shell-storm that turns his Cataphractii plate into a lightshow of sparks.

'Pattern: Praetego,' Urcus orders, his armoured back to the pillar and lightning claws crackling in expectation. Nereon and Eurotas have made it to pillars and are returning fire with their combi-bolters. Pontus assumes position in the statuesque architecture of the chamber wall, his heavy flamer ready to answer the call when the range is right.

Assault cannon fire chews away at the pillars, showering the Ultramarines with grit. Within moments Squad Urcus is confronted with another problem. Urcus hears it first: the distinctive bark of boltguns. Squinting through the raining masonry and stellar brilliance, he sees Word Bearers moving out of the side vestibules. The Ultramarines lay down judicious fire from cover.

'Circe's rings!' the sergeant curses. The enemy have them. 'Pattern: Vorto.'

Instead of taking cover behind the pillars, the Ultramarines are forced to work their way around. Streams of bolter fire rip into the architecture around them, showering the Terminators in grit and dust. Urcus hears the *whoosh* of a flamer in the blinding brilliance and moves around between two pillars. He finds himself facing Eurotas, who is similarly taking cover from the advancing Word Bearers on the other side of the chamber. A gout of flame hits the sergeant's pillar, spreading out about the stone.

'Eurotas,' Urcus says, as the fiery tendrils of flame stream around to reach for him. The battle-brother leans out in his Cataphractii plate. He has a better angle on the Word Bearers beyond and the benefit of auto-senses and targeters. Allowing the nebulous gout of flame to disappear, Brother Eurotas hammers several short bursts of bolter fire into the foe. He hits him in the chest, pauldron and weapon. As the bolts hit the promethium tank beneath, the flamer detonates, blasting the Word Bearer to shreds and enveloping two of his compatriots in a blanket of fiery death.

'Pattern: Motem,' Urcus urges. The Contemptor's assault cannon is back, tearing back and forth across the pillars and the spaces in between. Caught in the crossfire, even with the cover offered by the nest of support columns, the Ultramarines are forced to keep moving.

The chamber shakes. At first Urcus thinks it is an aftershock from the flamer detonation. Scraping his back armour around the stone pillar, the sergeant realises that the quake he can feel through the floor is the Dreadnought. The Word Bearers war machine charges. The chunky hydraulics of its legs power its bulk across the chamber, its assault cannon raging with rotary gunfire.

Urcus readies his claws, pulsing energies down between the blades like arcs between reactor power nodes. The Dreadnought doesn't stop, however. Shattering the stone floor with each heavy step, the monstrous thing hits the sergeant's pillar with an armoured shoulder. The column smashes. Urcus is battered from his feet, great stone fragments tumbling with him. The sergeant staggers away with the momentum of the impact, desperate not to fall. As he tries to turn, his boots skid across the floor. Bending his knees he stabs his crackling claws into the stone, slowing himself to a crouching stop.

The Dreadnought staggers too. Its great metal feet struggle about the stump of the column. As it rights itself, chunks of rock fall from the chamber ceiling and bounce off its plate.

Amidst the blaze of the stellar storm and the cloud of rock dust, Brother Eurotas opens fire, drilling into the Dreadnought's chest and helm with his combi-bolter. For a moment the metal monster is showered with ricochets. Eurotas steps closer, pressing his advantage with the twin barrels of his weapon held high. A storm of sparks emerges from the Dreadnought's huge power fist. The sergeant pushes up off his claws, thundering at the Contemptor, but it is too late.

The crackling fist's first impact strikes Eurotas like the prow of a ramming strike cruiser. Caught between the Dreadnought's fist and a stone pillar, his Cataphractii plate crumples like foil. Rents rip through the ceramite layers of his suit, and servos buckle. The Ultramarine's helm splits open. Eurotas totters back at the monstrous machine in a daze, dropping his combi-bolter and reaching out blindly with his own crackling gauntlet. The Dreadnought grabs Eurotas about his chest, the thick digits of its power fist holding the Ultramarine in a crushing grip.

Heaving Eurotas and the dead weight of his armoured suit from the floor, the Dreadnought holds him there. Urcus is but several rattling steps away, the bolt-rounds of Word Bearers cutting through the air about him.

The Cataphractii suit drags Urcus down like an anchor, refusing to answer the urgency in his hearts. The Dreadnought turns to face the oncoming sergeant, Eurotas now merely an afterthought. The machine fires off the stubby barrels of its combi-bolter, situated in the palm of its crushing fist. The rounds tear straight through Eurotas, producing a woeful moan from the dazed warrior. Engaging the full power of its monstrous fist in one pulverising contraction, the Dreadnought crushes the Terminator suit like a rations can. Gore explodes from the fatal grip, cascading to the ground in an ugly splatter.

Urcus roars, throwing himself at the Dreadnought. Slamming into it with his buckled pauldron, the sergeant knocks it back. Dropping Eurotas's crushed corpse, the dread machine stumbles off-balance. The Dreadnought thrusts the barrels of its assault cannon at Urcus and the sergeant hears the rotary mechanism hum to life. Pivoting out of the path of the weapon's devastating shellstorm, Urcus slams his claws through the cannon's weapons cradle. With the criss-crossed blades impaling the arm mechanism, Urcus angles the blazing assault cannon around, sending a devastating stream of fire into a throng of emboldened and advancing Word Bearers.

Another group press their advantage from the opposite side vestibule, their merciless boltfire punching through Brother

Nereon. As the Ultramarine crashes to his knees, more bolts pluck away at him – one finding its way through an eye-lens and into his brain. With a plate-clattering shudder, Nereon falls face-first onto the floor.

As the Word Bearers rush forwards to claim his corpse, they are lost in a bank of flame. Brother Pontus steps out from the busy architecture of the chamber wall, ready to avenge his brother. The inferno streaming from his heavy flamer engulfs the emerging Word Bearers, sending them stumbling and falling in blazing agony.

'Fall back,' Urcus commands. The trap has been sprung. The slaughter consolidated. The Dreadnought unleashed upon Squad Urcus and the squad decimated. Andron Pontus will not abandon his sergeant, however, and strides forwards, presenting the scorched muzzles of his heavy flamer.

The Dreadnought turns with hydraulic savagery, swinging Urcus with it. His claws slip from their purchase, wrenched free of the weapons cradle. Urcus spins with the momentum, coming around to face the Dreadnought's back. Slashing with his crackling claws, the sergeant cuts through the ammunition belt feeding the assault cannon from a shoulder-mounted ammunition store. Shells cascade to the floor and the assault cannon stutters to a stop.

Urcus goes to bury his lightning claws in the Dreadnought's back but the machine is a whirlwind of weaponry. Bringing the heavy assault cannon barrel back at Urcus like a club, the Dreadnought almost caves his skull in. Heaving back and leaning the bulk of his suit out of the cannon's path, Urcus slashes with his lightning claws. Left. Right. Left. The Dreadnought engages in an awkward retreat, stepping back through Brother Nereon's remains with the sizzling gashes of the sergeant's searing blades running through its thick chest-mounted plate.

'Come on!' Urcus bellows at the deranged machine. It swings for him in response, the ponderous arc of its colossal power fist just missing the sergeant. Urcus backslashes with his left claw, cutting into the armour on the back of the crackling fist. Stomping forwards, the sergeant makes his move. Manoeuvring in dangerously close to the manic machine, Urcus lays a lightning claw on its huge chest, rearing back with the other like a scorpion.

Before Urcus can thrust his claw into the vile machine, the Dreadnought lifts a leg and stamps at his armoured chest. The force is horrendous. Urcus feels his breastplate give way. His chest carapace cracks and several reinforced ribs shatter. The kick sends Urcus reeling. Pillars seem to blur past him until he strikes one and staggers off to one side. He hits the stone floor of the chamber, joining the corpses of Ultramarines already slain by the monstrous Dreadnought. Urcus skids along the blood-slick floor on his smashed chest, finally coming to rest.

The sergeant allows himself an excruciating breath.

Beyond, the Dreadnought has gone wild, punching through thick columns with its power fist. Snatching up a great piece of shattered masonry, the machine hurls the half-pillar at Brother Pontus. Urcus lifts his head; further agony. The colossal piece of rock hits the chamber wall, obliterating a sculpted representation of the primarch. As the dust clears, Urcus sees that a broken Andron Pontus lies behind it. The Terminator's side has been caved in and his armoured limbs are twisted and broken. His plate sparks from ceramite breaches and cabling that has snaked loose like entrails.

'Andron,' Urcus says, the word sharp with pain. Beyond, the sergeant can hear the Dreadnought thundering at him once more: an enraged metal bull charging through the maze of columns. 'Andron,' Urcus wheezes again.

Andron tries to look up. His helm is shattered and he holds his head at an unnatural angle. Beneath his chest, Urcus can feel the pounding step of the monstrous machine. Stabbing the tips of his lightning claws into the stone floor, he pushes himself up.

Pontus awkwardly shakes his head. 'Go...' he slurs across the static-riddled vox. 'Go!'

Orestrian Urcus forces his ramshackle suit of plate into a slow run. Pushing himself off one pillar then another, the sergeant surges back the way his squad had come. He turns between the stone columns as he goes, trying to build up enough momentum to outrun the Dreadnought, which is hammering its clunky way across the chamber.

Andron Pontus stretches out with the sparking stump of a mangled hand and gauntlet – reaching for the pool of shimmering promethium that has spilled about him from the ruptured flasks of his smashed heavy flamer. The stump sparks. The fuel takes. The flames spread.

An explosive *whoosh* swallows Brother Pontus and the Word Bearers Dreadnought. As the weapon detonates, blasting the Ultramarine apart, the machine is knocked off its pounding course through the flames and into several columns. The sergeant knows he must make the most of his squad's sacrifice. Forcing once leg on after another, Urcus leaves his decimated squad and the chamber behind.

'Command, this is Urcus. Respond,' the sergeant calls, his breath ragged. He is stomping down tunnels, through vaults and beneath blast doors. He waits for a response but there is nothing except the howl of static. He thinks on the intensity of the stellar storm outside, the radiation raging across the surface and bleeding in through reinforced openings and sabotaged entrances. Once more the Word Bearers have lured the Ultramarines in, but prevented them from summoning aid by making use of the communications disruption outside.

Urcus knows he has to reach the lower levels, to give his vox-transmitter a better chance of reaching the command nexus. He must warn Aethon and the Ultramarines about the Dreadnought and the slaughter. He must warn his captain that regardless of his offer to Kurtha Sedd, the Word Bearers are making their move. Taking back territories in the underworld newly established by the sons of Guilliman – leaving ash and armoured corpses in their wake.

'Command, this is Sergeant Urcus,' he says, hammering his way down colonnaded passageways and pipe-lined access tunnels. As the rhythmic rattle of his ruined plate echoes about the undervaults and arcology chambers, he knows the monstrous Dreadnought is hunting him through the underworld, spurred on by hatred.

Urcus slows. His plate is giving him away. As he moves more cautiously through the arcology network, down through the system levels, he hears the Dreadnought searching chambers and forking tunnels. Like some hulking predator of the death world plains, it is economical in its search and relentless in its pursuit. It can smell him – it can smell the honour of his plate, the nobility of his primarch's blood, his loyalty and his genic fortitude.

The sergeant slows the exhausted thud of his steps and puts

his back to a wall. He can hear the Dreadnought nearby, the thunder of its movements as it hunts him through the labyrinthine chambers and rough corridors. Urcus closes his eyes for a moment. Behind them, the battlefields of Melior-Tertia wait for him. There the heavy metal movements of the Dreadnought tearing through neighbouring chambers becomes the dreadful mechanical clunk of augmented aliens...

'Aethon!' Urcus roars. 'Aethon!'

They have become separated. The explosion, brighter than the sun. Hitting them like a blizzard of invisible hammers on their Mark III plate. The detonation had been something crude and orbital. Something visited upon the Ultramarines formations by a closing hulk or greenskin terror ship. Perhaps even an alien vessel itself, slamming into the frozen factory world's surface on a suicide run.

'Aethon!'

The squad is gone. Urcus finds himself standing in bubbling water. The snowdrifts half burying the Mechanicum forge temples have melted about him. Within moments ice has turned to meltwater and meltwater begun to boil. There are armoured bodies in the shallows. A carpet of plate, blue and grey. Dead Ultramarines, dead Word Bearers. Warriors everywhere. Urcus stumbles through the carnage, searching the shallows for his sergeant and squad in the bodies below.

The greenskins stomp through the dirty steam. Bulky shadows at first, moving with the mechanical jerkiness of brute hydraulics. As the steam clears, they materialise properly. The greenskin warrior elite, buried inside small walking tanks of thick armour. Monstrous pneumatic pincers. Plate-mounted weaponry, launchers and rockets. Hasty paint jobs and tribal markings. It had been rich pickings in the Melior-Corpus for the alien invaders: Mechanicum factory worlds to pillage and strip for their technological wonders. Assembly-line resources finding new purpose in greenskin workshops.

The Ultramarines find their order once more. Space Marines rally to their officers. The chatter of boltguns attempts to reassert itself but the greenskins in their heavy exoskeletal suits blast crude rockets from arm-mountings. The rockets shriek away into the Space Marines splashing through the shallows.

Urcus spots his sergeant. He has landed some distance away. The White Spider is a stumbling figure in dripping plate. Weaponless. Disorientated. Rising from the waters to stagger this way and that. At the enemy. Away from them. Urcus lifts his boltgun but he is out of range.

He runs through the water towards his sergeant, watching with dread as an augmented greenskin chieftain in a small mountain of plate stomps towards Aethon through the steaming shallows. The monster's weapon carriages bear a pair of heavy circular saws that spit and thrash at the surface of the water.

'Aethon!' Urcus calls, but the sergeant does not seem to hear him, across either the vox-channel or the submerged battlefield. Urcus keeps stopping to fire off streams of shot at the walking fortress. Glancing bolt-rounds shower the armoured alien but the thing will not be distracted. Bolt-rounds are for the mindless monster's armoured suit to worry about. The towering greenskin wishes to sate its barbarian's wrath on the dazed warrior before it, stumbling stunned through the shallows.

It guns the circular killsaws raging at the end of each mechanised arm. Aethon claws his way through the water, away from the flesh-shredding blades. Desperately trying to get to his feet, he tears a metal rod from the submerged bionics of a dead alien. Aethon puts the metal shaft between him and the mulching killsaws, and

Urcus sees his sergeant showered in sparks and then wrenched off his feet. The rod flies off in one direction, while Aethon is sent flying backwards into the water by the ringing contact.

Urcus watches his friend surface, just in time for the killing blow. The greenskin beast lifts a buzzing killsaw and brings it down on the Ultramarines sergeant with as much brute mechanical force as the ramshackle alien suit can muster.

'No!' Urcus yells, his footsteps kicking up fountains of meltwater about him. His movements feel leaden and slow. He will not make it in time. He–

The air rings with the sound of metal on metal, the saw blade turned aside by a crackling energy field. Aethon is dazed but alive, trying to get up out of the shallows. Between him and the armoured monster, Urcus sees a Word Bearer.

A Chaplain. Kurtha Sedd.

The head of his crozius arcanum hurtles up at the raging greenskin brute, knocking its spinning, circular blades aside once more. Urcus sprints through the shallows with as much speed as his plate will permit. Every second is another murderous lunge the Chaplain has to deflect. Another death-defying moment spent under the storm of the greenskin's powered blows.

Urcus slams into the monster, his pauldron crumpling against the heavy metal frame of the suit's gut. The impact is enough to unbalance the thing, however, and the beast goes over on its side, sending an almighty splash up into the gelid air. Urcus looks up to see Kurtha Sedd standing over them both. The Chaplain lifts his crozius like a hero of legend slaying some mythical monster, and brings it down with such elegant force that Urcus flinches and looks away.

Meltwater clouds to a bloody miasma around the alien beast as Kurtha Sedd smashes the spiked globe of the crozius into its face. Shrapnel and rude workings fountain up with each terrible blow, accompanied by blood, skull and brains. His armoured chest rising and falling with the exertion, the Chaplain stops, his gore-dribbling rod of office held high.

Urcus risks a glance at the ruined skull-shell of the beast. Kurtha Sedd has annihilated the monstrous creature. Urcus stands in the bloody waters, sloshing across to his sergeant, who is attempting to stand. Aethon's plate is a ragged wreck. His helm is smashed, the flesh beneath flash-scarred and livid with blood pouring from a gash above one eye.

'Get him up,' Kurtha Sedd says, backing towards them. All around, clunking through the steam, Urcus can hear pistons and hydraulics, the rumble of combustion engines and the shriek of killsaws. Greenskins close on them in their monstrous armoured suits. Standing over the two Ultramarines, the Chaplain slips his plasma pistol from its holster. 'Your sidearm,' Kurtha Sedd says to Urcus, prompting him to draw his own bolt pistol. The pair give the pistols to the unsteady Aethon.

'Flask and magazine are full,' Urcus shouts, looking into his friend's dazed eyes. He isn't sure if Aethon can hear after the explosion but is swiftly rewarded with a jerky nod.

As alien monsters in their exoskeletal suits surround them, Urcus ejects the empty magazine from his boltgun and slams another into the breech. Kneeling in the shallows next to Aethon, he primes the weapon. Kurtha Sedd towers over them, swinging the crozius arcanum in a terrible arc of gore-streaming death.

'Make them pay,' the Chaplain orders. 'For the price of opposing the Emperor of Mankind is a dear one.'

ORESTRIAN URCUS NODS his head. He sniffs and blinks the memory from his eyes. The price will be dear indeed – for

Kurtha Sedd and his Word Bearer mongrels. The Dreadnought is closing. He can hear its immense footfalls in the
tunnel beyond. Whether it knows it or not, the monstrous
machine has found him.

Urcus makes a break for it, driving his shattered Cataphractii suit on through the darkness of the pillared vault. The
Dreadnought erupts from the tunnel opening, the pistons
of its legs working with relentless fury to carry the thing's
bulk through the chamber. Armoured feet smash the stone
beneath it, while the Dreadnought holds its power fist out,
chunky digits reaching for the escaping Ultramarine. It isn't
attempting to grab him, however.

Urcus feels the drum of bolt-rounds cutting through his
smashed plate. Bolts shot from the barrels set within the power
fist's palm hammer through his pauldron and shoulder, almost
spinning him off his feet. The Terminator sergeant staggers
to one side, pushing himself from pillar to pillar. The pain
is excruciating and his arm feels numb. With the thunder of
the machine's furious approach bouncing about the chamber,
Urcus puts as much masonry between him and the Dreadnought as he can, before approaching an open blast door.

The sergeant recognises the markings on it as those belonging to the Proprium-Termini. Slashing a lightning claw
through the blast-door controls, Urcus backs beneath the
broad bulkhead as it judders towards the floor. As he retreats
from the entrance he hears the Contemptor charge, burying its mighty power fist in the door. The metal buckles and
crackling arcs of power dance briefly across its creased surface. Scraping his claw along the wall, Urcus stumbles away.
All about him the tunnel booms with the impacts of the
Dreadnought's fist.

As Urcus surges on, his armour like an anchor to be dragged along with him, he listens to the Dreadnought's attacks growing ever more furious. Finally, with an excruciating sound, the blast door gives way. The tunnel seems to stretch on into eternity. With the Contemptor thundering up behind, Urcus begins to doubt that he will make it. Bolt-rounds pluck at the rough stone of the tunnel wall and plough lines of craters into the floor at his feet. Optimistic blasts, perhaps, but with each stumbling step, the Dreadnought closes the weapon's range.

'Urcus to Command,' he voxes, hoping that the interference from the stellar storm will be less at such levels. 'Urcus to Command – please respond.'

Nothing. No response. No static. Nothing. As Urcus claws his way up the passage, the Dreadnought's gunfire rattling past in savage streams, the channel suddenly chirps with recognition.

'Sergeant Urcus, this is Sergeant Fidos Galtarion,' a voice returns. 'We have you and your target in our sights.'

Urcus peers ahead. Through the murk he can make out two power-armoured legionaries standing sentinel at the end of the tunnel: Ultramarines charged with the security of the depot and cargo teleportarium beyond.

'Galtarion, you don't–'

'Stand to one side, sergeant,' Galtarion tells him before the Ultramarines guards open fire. Stumbling along the wall, Urcus allows the bolter fire to rip through the air next to him. He can hear the impact of rounds drumming off the Contemptor's plate. Within moments, the metal monster has new targets and sends hails of bolts back at the Ultramarines.

'Galtarion,' Urcus warns. 'We must fall back.'

'My orders are to hold this facility,' Fidos Galtarion tells him across the vox amidst the crash of gunfire. 'My captain's orders. And that's exactly what I'm going to–'

A bolt-round takes the sergeant in the head, his helm blown clean off. Urcus shoves past the armoured body as it crashes to the floor.

'Legionary?' Urcus roars at the second warrior.

'Nysus, brother-sergeant,' the Ultramarine answers.

'Fall back, Brother Nysus!'

'Yes, brother-sergeant,' Nysus says, reaching for his commander's abandoned boltgun and its precious ammunition.

'Leave it,' Urcus orders, stomping into the cargo depot. Spraying the tunnel with a last hailstorm of bolter fire, Nysus follows. The Dreadnought's crazed blasting follows them through the demolished stacks, tearing through cargo.

'Last one,' Nysus says, as Urcus rounds the corner into the teleportarium corridor. He hammers home another magazine, primes his boltgun and blasts a stream of fire back at the Contemptor.

'Get inside,' Urcus snaps as the Word Bearers machine smashes through barrels, cargo crates and toppled webbing stacks. Cracking off a final couple of rounds, Brother Nysus steps through the doorway. Punching his crackling claw into the teleportarium door controls, Urcus prompts the heavy bulkhead to crash down to the floor. 'Can you work this damnable thing?' Urcus asks as the pair of them make for the teleportarium chamber.

'As well as anyone else,' Nysus says. He doesn't sound confident. 'It's not a precision piece of equipment.'

As Urcus rattles his way along the short corridor and into the chamber, Nysus enters the control booth. The sergeant climbs up onto the translation slab. While Nysus engages the teleporter mechanism and the reactors fire up, the sergeant listens to the resounding *boom* of the Word Bearers Dreadnought punching its way through to them.

'Just get us to the command nexus,' Urcus orders as Nysus engages the translation sequence. Rushing up onto the slab, Nysus joins the Terminator sergeant.

'I can guarantee that part will happen,' Nysus tells him. 'In what form we will arrive there, I cannot say.'

The Ultramarines wait. And wait. Urcus can hear the cacophonous yielding of contorted metal. The Dreadnought is done with the bulkhead and is stomping up the passage towards the teleportarium.

Lights are flashing. Klaxons fill the small chamber with heart-stopping urgency. Urcus sees the nightmarish machine round the corner, the bulk of its crimson plate lit up briefly in the flashing strobes.

'I thought you said you could guarantee–'

Translation initiates. The Dreadnought reaches out for them with the outstretched claw of its power fist. Bolter fire rages from the palm of the weapon. Urcus turns his head away, but the leaden mists of translation have already descended. He closes his eyes. A vertiginous feeling of falling in every direction at once rolls through him. His stomach turns. His mind aches. Pain wracks his body. The dreadful feeling of translation seems to span an unbearable age, while in fact lasting only a second or two.

Opening his eyes, Urcus finds himself in a larger teleportarium. A metallic steam dissipates. The thunder of the approaching Dreadnought is gone.

He turns to face Brother Nysus only to see his battle-brother crash to his knees and fall faceplate-first onto the translation slab. Smoking craters in his armour show where the Word Bearers machine managed to punch through him with its fire.

With sudden urgency, Urcus steps down from the slab and approaches the control booth. It is empty. Bringing a lightning claw to a crackling nimbus of arcing power, the sergeant sinks the stabbing blades into the metal of the booth and runs the weapon along its length. He has no intention of letting the Dreadnought follow them through to wreak havoc in the command nexus. Having ripped the workings out of the teleportarium controls, Urcus turns to face the translation slab and the body of Nysus.

'Be at peace, brother,' Urcus says gently.

Only then does he hear the sound of gunfire beyond the teleportarium door. A rumble passes through the chamber. Urcus feels the ground quake beneath his boots. Dust rains from the rocky ceiling. He totters and reaches out for the wall, only to find it shuddering also. After a moment, the distant thunder passes and the chamber grows still. The sergeant reasons that the quake must be subterranean in nature, rather than the localised detonations of missiles or grenades. The sections above and about the command nexus are collapsing. He looks up at the trembling ceiling and then back at Nysus.

Here on this benighted world, where every shadow hides a traitor, there is precious little peace to be had.

NINE

[mark: 136.53.13]

'WHAT BEWITCHMENT IS this?' Acting Sergeant Dardanus asks.

A living darkness fills the underworld tunnels through which he moves. It caresses his bolt-cratered plate with the hiss and spark of a satin static. Its touch is something unnatural, an otherworldly phenomenon such as Dardanus has never before experienced. As they have descended through the arcology systems, down through the under-vaults, the sub-levels and into the depths, the miasmic gloom has risen to meet them. Like a river of darkness it flows through the natural tunnels and fractures of the underworld, filling the unexplored caverns with its black-ness and dread, spuming up from the bowels of the planet like a toxic fume.

'Hadriax?'

Dardanus asks the legionary, a native of Calth, for his opinion. The Ultramarine holds his heavy bolter in close, sweeping the gaping barrels of the weapon left and right through the gloom.

'I've seen strange things in the arcology systems and the sub-levels below,' Hadriax admits. 'Piezoelectrical disturbances. Labyrinths that can turn a man about and swallow him whole. Things that creep, crawl and glow in the depths. I have never seen anything like this.'

'Tibor?'

'No,' Tibor answers, attempting to recoil from the murk. As he does so the gloom seems to close on him with a near-sentient interest and for a moment the legionary is lost. 'Filters, auspectrals, nothing.'

'So it's not a technological effect or a natural phenomenon. Brother Aloysio,' Dardanus says. 'Care to enlighten us?'

'You know I cannot do that, acting sergeant,' Aloysio says, his movements wary as Squad Sephirus makes its way down the rough tunnel.

'So it is something… else,' Dardanus says, ducking beneath a rocky outcrop. The acting sergeant hears a dark chuckle from behind them, the voice of one of the Word Bearer prisoners. Dardanus turns, bringing the column to a standstill. Brother Envixus halts with his boltgun buried in the Word Bearer's back.

'You have something to say, Colchisian?' Dardanus says, leaning in.

'You analyse and measure,' the Word Bearer laughs at his captor. 'You reference and enquire. How like the frightened children of Ultramar. How like Guilliman's weakling breed.'

'Enlighten us,' Dardanus says, leaning in closer. 'Bearer of the Word.'

The traitor's smirk contorts into something altogether more ugly.

'How can you hope to understand that for which even your cowardly witchbreed has no words? Aye, Ultramarine. We bear the words, for we fear them not. Not their utterance. Not their meaning. Not the knowledge carried through the ages in their letters and syllables.'

'Speak them now, traitor,' Dardanus challenges the prisoner, as the living darkness smothers him. The tendrils of inky shadow try to feel their way into his power armour.

'I will,' the prisoner spits back. 'If only to hear the dread-laced quiver of your own. The darkness is a Legion at my master's command. It is a shield behind which all sons of Colchis wait for you. It is a weapon crafted of fear itself, to which no being of self and soul is immune. It is your end, Ultramarine, closing in to meet you. The blackness that creeps from the corner of your eye. The closing of the sarcophagus lid. The sun suddenly extinguished in the daytime sky. It is doom and it is death.'

Arkan Dardanus turns his helm to Brother Envixus.

'Could the traitor be more vague?' he says. 'Your corpse will be at our feet soon enough, Word Bearer. For now you have a duty to perform. The last honourable one you will ever be given.'

'What would you have me do?' the traitor asks, mocking, before descending into ragged laughter.

'I would have you live, you mongrel,' Dardanus tells him. 'Think you can manage that? I would have you crawl back into the pit whence you came and report to your Chaplain, Kurtha Sedd. I would have you give him my captain's message.'

'I'll deliver his message,' the Word Bearer tells him, 'but expect one in return, Ultramarine, for my master will answer in blood–'

'Targets,' Hadriax hisses across the vox.

The Word Bearer chuckles darkly.

'Back,' Dardanus orders.

'In here,' Tibor says, pulling his own prisoner back into a cavern opening they have just passed.

'Go,' the acting sergeant agrees.

Tibor slips through the narrow, craggy opening with the limping traitor, disappearing into the swirling darkness inside. Envixus backs in, his boltgun still aimed at the head of the Word Bearer with whom Dardanus had been speaking.

He almost collides with Brother Aloysio, who approaches the cavern with hesitation. There is no time for caution, however. As Hadriax retreats from the oncoming enemy targets, Dardanus grabs the prisoner by the top lip of his breastplate and hurls him around. Thrusting him into the opening with the momentum of the turn, the acting sergeant marches him back. With Hadriax and his heavy bolter now bringing up the rear, the Ultramarines take positions just inside the rocky entrance.

Snapping off suit lamps and dimming their eye-lenses, Squad Sephirus wait in the absolute darkness of the cavern, their boltguns aimed through the narrow opening at the tunnel beyond. Brother Hadriax takes one side with his monstrous weapon, ready to blast apart any legionary unwise enough to investigate the opening. Dardanus takes the other side, his prisoner slammed back against the rough wall, a drawn bolt pistol aimed between the mad sparkle of the Word Bearer's eyes.

'I can smell your fear,' the traitor whispers as the ceramite
rattle of an approaching column of Word Bearers fills the
tunnel. 'You would do well to let us go, Ultramarine. I think
this is as far into the depths as you dare venture.'

Dardanus stares at the leering Word Bearer's face through
the false-colour static of his night-vision filters. He drifts
the bolt pistol's barrel down the legionary's face, moving
his mask aside with the curve of the weapon's magazine. As
the Word Bearer goes to speak, the acting sergeant crams the
muzzle of the bolt pistol into the traitor's mouth, breaking
a tooth and slamming his head back against the rock. Blood
leaks from the corner of his lips.

About the barrel, the traitor smiles. The alerting sound of a
ragged chuckle begins to build in his chest. Dardanus snarls
within his helm. Bringing the bolt pistol up, he smashes
the grip down on the Word Bearer's shaven skull. A sickening thud and a scrape of plate later, Brother Envixus has the
unconscious Space Marine in his arms, allowing Dardanus
to move forwards.

Watching through a crook in the rocky opening, the acting sergeant sees a never-ending column of Word Bearers
stream by. It is as though they are one with the living darkness. They seem at once part of reality and divorced from it,
the gloom like an otherworldly beast obscuring them with
its nightmare form. Dardanus can only imagine that Lorgar
Aurelian and his treacherous sons have left the enlightened
path of the Great Crusade, of the Imperium, of the Emperor
to pursue dark talents long banished from the ranks of the
Ultramarines.

Dardanus tears his gaze from the crimson-clad column of
Word Bearers streaming forth like a spectral army from the

depths. They seem carried along by the torrent of sentient darkness. He looks at Saraman Aloysio and sees the glint of a knife in the gloom. A blade that bleeds forth from the darkness, settling its razored edge into the groove between Aloysio's helm and breastplate.

The acting sergeant can only watch in horror. He brings his pistol around and opens his lips to voice warning. Not before the knife flashes suddenly to one side, like the whip of a scorpion's tail, slipping between the seals and through the sinewed flesh of the Ultramarine's throat. Blood sprays, vaulting through the gloom like a fountain to bespeckle the members of Squad Sephirus.

Within moments, it is over. Cloaked by the living darkness of the underworld cavern, Word Bearers assassins snatch, slash and stab the hiding Ultramarines. The great heavy bolter comes around to meet the threat but Brother Hadriax's ceramite fingertip never gets to haul back on the trigger. A blade slams into the side of his helm, squealing through the bone of his skull before emerging out of the other side to spark off the stone of the wall. Stricken and still, Hadriax stands there for a moment before crashing to the floor.

Envixus is grabbed from behind and torn back into the murk. As he disappears, Dardanus makes out the impression of a crimson arm about his neck and another burying a knife in the Ultramarine's chest. Dardanus fires off a couple of shots, dropping Brother Envixus's killer and another shadowy figure venturing from the gloom.

Iolchus Tibor gets his boltgun around and manages to blast off a single shot before the weapon is batted to one side. A Word Bearer thrusts a tapering blade at Tibor, stabbing straight through his faceplate grille and into his head. Tibor stumbles back, slamming his pack into the rough wall before firing off another couple of bolts into the cavern floor. With that, the Ultramarine slides down onto the ground to die.

Dardanus's bolt pistol crashes several more times into the darkness. He cannot be sure he is hitting anything, the enemy obscured by the supernatural blackness. The pistol's magazine is but half full and within moments is spent. As the empty *clunk* of the weapon echoes about the cavern, feverish green eye-lenses burn once again to intensity in the gloom.

Arkan Dardanus can feel his heart in his throat. The cavern is a constellation of burning green stars. More Word Bearers than one solitary Ultramarine can ever hope to vanquish. It does not stop him from trying, though. Allowing the pistol to tumble from his gauntlet and clatter to the floor, the acting sergeant reaches for the heavy bolter that lies nearby, still in Brother Hadriax's spasming grip.

'Alive…' a voice reaches out from the sentient gloom. 'I want the last of them alive.'

As Dardanus lays his hands on the heavy weapon, he feels arms and gauntlets latch onto him. The enemy are all about him. Their knives are sheathed and boltguns mag-locked to their belts. Dardanus struggles and reaches out for one but is wrenched back. The Ultramarine pulls on all the engineered strength of his form and plate, but with two Word Bearers on each arm and another wrangling him about the waist, he is held immobile.

As his struggles subside and his remaining weaponry is stripped from his belt, Dardanus hears the crunch of grit beneath armoured boots. A pair of green lenses sizzle through the dread blackness towards him. His helm is removed with the hiss of clearance and Dardanus blinks the darkness from his eyes.

'Lamps.' It is the same voice, issuing orders laced with unquestioned authority. The stabbing, Colchisian-accented syllables are smeared into a phantasmal drone by the super-natural gloom. Suit lamps cut through the murk, wavering before settling on Dardanus's face.

The cavern is a sea of shadowy silhouettes. The outlines of traitors in dishonoured plate. Before Dardanus is a Word Bearers officer – no, a Chaplain. Even with his shape cut out of the blazing light of the lamps, Dardanus can make out the cloak, the helm plume and the Chaplain's imposing staff of office. He clutches it like a great axe or warhammer in his gauntlet. Like his surrounding Word Bearers, the Chaplain shimmers with the unnatural gloom, the darkness seeming to react with a static hiss and flickering at the light. His eye-lenses burn the green of bottomless envy and greed, while a plasma pistol glows blue death on his belt. The sigils and scripture adorning the Chaplain's plate seethe their desire to be read with infernal brilliance.

'Name and rank,' the Chaplain demands.

Dardanus tries to turn his head but a gauntlet settles on his shaven crown, holding him in place. Holding his gaze on the light – on the Chaplain. Dardanus does not reply.

'Your name, Ultramarine,' the Chaplain says again, with abyssal patience.

'His name is Dardanus.'

Dardanus recognises the voice of his prisoner. His words are slurred from concussion, but the Word Bearer has been revived by his brothers. The prisoners now stand where Aethon had intended them: back in the ranks of the enemy. Dardanus has achieved that much at least. 'Acting sergeant.'

'Field promotions,' the Chaplain observes with a delighted hiss. 'We must be hitting their officer corps harder than we thought.'

'There's more,' another prisoner offers, eager to exonerate his own failure at being captured. Dardanus can feel his hatred. 'They are led by a captain. He gave his name as Steloc Aethon.'

'The Honoured, of course,' the Chaplain chuckles with venom. Something about the name seems to amuse him. 'Aethon, my old friend. It is I who am honoured. Honoured to have lost so many of my kindred – not to any warrior of Ultramar, but to Steloc Aethon – the noble son of a doomed world. A world with an ignoble end.

'Aethon, Aethon, Aethon. I thought it was you… I hoped it wasn't, and then prayed it was. For you of all Guilliman's lowly warriors, should know what it is to drown in your own shadow. To sink into a darkness all of your own and find the ocean of possibility waiting for you there. For the shadow is the shore upon which the true enlightenment crashes, waiting to claim you with the current of its undeniable logic. Its primordial truth. You will not find such understanding in Macragge's dusty libraries, Ultramarine, or the tactical amphitheatres of your Legion's mighty vessels.'

'So the Urizen's breed truly have lost their minds and their way,' Dardanus returns.

The Chaplain chuckles deep within his helm. 'Toc Derenoth?' he prompts.

'This Aethon…' the prisoner says.

'Your captor,' the Chaplain reminds him, with a dark edge to his words.

'He set us free,' Toc Derenoth continues.

'He set you free?' the Chaplain marvels. 'And yet I find you here with legionaries unworthy of a primarch's blood.'

'It was this wretch's responsibility to return me to the depths,' Toc Derenoth says. 'To you, Chaplain – with a message.'

'Then you must be the piece of traitor filth known as Kurtha Sedd,' Dardanus says.

The Word Bearers close about him, tightening their grip in anger and reaching for their knives from their belts.

'Wait!' the Chaplain orders and the Word Bearers settle down. 'Not yet. A message?'

'He claims you were friends once,' Toc Derenoth says, 'and claims you as friend still. He alludes to a debt of blood that exists between you both. He wishes to speak with you. Send me back, Brother-Chaplain. I can deliver this Aethon for you. Without the loss of our kindred brothers.'

Dardanus watches the silhouette of Kurtha Sedd grow still, thoughtful. His helm bows, his gaze drifting to the floor, and his pauldrons sag with some great weight or consequence.

'Chaplain?' Toc Derenoth presses.

Darkness swirls about the Chaplain and the scripture of his plate glows like the dying embers of a smouldering brazier. He seems to be speaking to himself, thoughts falling from bitter lips within the privacy and confines of his helm.

'Aethon, Aethon – my old friend,' Kurtha Sedd says suddenly. Then, pointing the head of his crozius at Toc Derenoth:

'There is always blood, my brother, and loss is simply the price to be paid.'

Once again, the Chaplain seems lost in his dark thoughts. A distant rumble disturbs him. He turns his head. It sounds like a quake radiating down from the planet's surface, or a structural failure in one of the sub-arcologies.

He turns the crozius on Dardanus, using the head of the weapon to lift the Ultramarine's chin. 'You hear that, Ultramarine? That is the sound of your world – your very existence – collapsing about you. Your Emperor, your crusade and the Imperium are all beyond your reach now. All that awaits you now are the depths, the darkness, the Word and those who bear it. You will go back to your captain and tell him that Kurtha Sedd is eager to see him. We will receive him and see what he has to offer.'

'I don't take orders from the likes of you, traitor,' Dardanus spits.

'Of course,' Kurtha Sedd agrees. 'You already have your orders – don't you, Acting Sergeant Dardanus? To traverse the depths and make contact with Tetrarch Nicodemus over in the Magnesi arcology system.'

Dardanus tries to hide his surprise. Kurtha Sedd and his Word Bearers have done more than just cut off communications between the two arcology networks: they must have been monitoring them and drawing conclusions.

The Chaplain enjoys the realisation crossing the sergeant's features. He draws in close. The legionaries' breastplates brush, and Kurtha Sedd whispers in his ear. 'Don't worry about the Tetrarch. My brother Ungol Shax and his warriors keep him busy. Besides, you are about to pass the point of no return – you know, sergeant, the boundary beyond which it is further to return than press on. Believe me, my men and I know a great deal about breaching such boundaries. Trust me when I say that you are not ready…'

Dardanus feels the knife go in, a long blade that the Chaplain has thrust into his body. Kurtha Sedd has punched through plate and cabling, straight into Dardanus's stomach with a single stroke of maniacal hatred. The metal burns within his belly. It is pure agony and horror. Shock spreads like a numbing sensation out from the wound. Something else is wrong. Dardanus senses that the blade has nicked into his spine.

Then, with a fury hard to imagine even in a warrior of the Legiones Astartes, Kurtha Sedd tears the knife to one side. The sacrificial blade rips through plate, muscle and innards, tearing a ragged gash that leaves Dardanus all but cut in half.

The Word Bearers release him and step back as gore and intestines spill out of the legionary. Dardanus falls. It is not merely the shock. He has lost the use of his legs. He crashes back against the wall and falls to one side. His eyes are wide and his pupils dilated. A puddle of gore begins to gather about him. The sergeant looks about, the shock spreading through him, claiming his movements and thoughts. He holds there, stricken, as if afraid to let go of the floor.

Beyond, Dardanus hears the vicious laughter of Toc Derenoth but he barely registers it. Kurtha Sedd leans in. He is cloaked in living darkness. Dardanus's awareness is dominated by the Chaplain's two blazing green eye-lenses, and a voice laden with doom.

'Bring your captain to me, Dardanus,' the Chaplain orders. 'Bring me Aethon of the Honoured Nineteenth.'

With that, the Chaplain is gone, claimed by the darkness.

Dardanus gets the impression of Word Bearers receding, descending and disappearing into some great depression in the cavern floor. Only Toc Derenoth remains, the sentient murk swirling about him.

'My corpse at *your* feet?' the Word Bearer says, mockingly echoing their exchange at the command nexus. 'I think not, Ultramarine. I think not.'

ARKAN DARDANUS DOES not know how long he lies there in his own blood and guts, his body numb with pain, his mind frozen with shock. Every action is an agony. Every movement prompts the small lake of gore about him to burst its banks, spreading further. He tries to think – to hold on to a single thought. He must go back. He must warn Aethon. He must give his brothers the location of their most hated foe.

He instinctively reaches out for a pistol, a boltgun, a knife. His gauntlet shakes and his plate rattles. Clenching a fist he thumps the ground in frustration. His legs will not answer. They are a deadweight, like the armour encasing them, to be dragged behind him. He cannot carry a weapon – he needs both hands, both arms, to drag himself along. He reaches out for his helm, which lies abandoned nearby. He scoops it up and slips it loosely over his head. He has neither the strength nor inclination to clasp the seals.

'Dar...'

He can barely manage to croak his own name. 'Dardanus. Command, come in.'

Reaching arm over arm, like a training initiate on an assault course, he hauls his body across the floor, leaving a river of blood behind him. The pain is incredible. A nova burns in the pit of his stomach. His arms are weak and he can't feel his legs at all. Using his armoured fingertips he crawls back the way he and Squad Sephirus have come.

His shock-addled mind struggles with the twists, turns and junctions of the labyrinthine underworld. At intersections he rests to regain his strength, and work out his route.

'Dardanus to Command,' he wheezes. 'Command, respond.'

He listens, but hears only static. Perhaps he is too deep. Perhaps it is interference from the surface, the supernatural gloom or something else. Dardanus's mind wrestles with the possibilities to keep him from thinking about other things. His life bleeding away behind him. His innards spilling out. The loss of his legs. An ignoble death stalking him through the maze of passageways and caverns.

Dardanus begins to fade. He doesn't know how far he has come. The smeared trail of gore could extend for kilometres behind him or he could barely have made it a few hundred metres. He could have been crawling in circles for hours, or be mere minutes from assistance. The sentient gloom grows denser about his wretched form. It seeps into his very being and drains his heart of hope.

Figures in crimson plate stream past through the dreamy murk. They march or jog past at intervals: squads of Word Bearers despatched from the depths to take the command nexus for their dread master, Kurtha Sedd.

Like a hunted animal Dardanus grows still. The Word Bearers can see his miserable form but they leave him alone. It is as though the darkness has already claimed the Ultramarine. Besides, the Chaplain has given his orders. Dardanus is not to be touched. Reasoning is a painful effort, but the Ultramarine comes to the conclusion that he is at least crawling the right way.

Beyond the silence there is thunder. Beyond the darkness, light. Dardanus can feel the rumble of some distant collapse through his plate and chest. Dust rains down onto his blood-soaked form. The tunnel shakes. Grit bounces before his eyes. It is the doom of which Kurtha Sedd spoke. The warriors of the Emperor – both loyal and traitor – are to be buried alive. Dardanus hears the excruciating crack and booming crunch of pulverised rock. Benighted passageways are suddenly lit up by funnelled flame, an inferno feeling its way down through breaches in the bedrock, the underworld and arcology net-works. The sergeant buries his helm in his hands as the fury of vented fire roars past, boiling the blood in his messy wake.

Dardanus crawls on. In a rare moment of clarity he finds that he is talking to himself. He does not know for how long he has been doing so, or whether he is making any sense.

'…they're all gone.'

He catches himself. He licks his dry lips. Thirst is a power-ful storm building up within him. Not a glorious monsoon or cloudburst but a sapping maelstrom of dust and desic-cated grit.

'…a trap.'

'*Dardanus, respond.*'

'…all dead.'

'*Sergeant, this is Captain Aethon,*' the open vox-channel crackles. '*Talk to me.*'

For the first time, Dardanus truly hears his captain. His words are punctuated by bolter fire. He guesses the com-mand nexus is once again under attack from Kurtha Sedd's Word Bearers.

'Captain?' he manages, his mind a shock-fractured and blood-drenched daze.

'*Sergeant,*' Aethon returns, his voice threaded with hope. '*Sergeant Dardanus, report status.*'

'Status?' Dardanus repeats back, fading in and out of consciousness. He stops crawling and with agonising effort rolls onto his side. He casts a skewed gaze down his suit. Past the ragged gash cut through his midriff plate and cabling. Down legs smeared with so much blood that the cobalt-blue brilliance of his armour can't be seen. A trail of blood stretches behind him.

'*Report your squad's status,*' Aethon orders, the captain clearly eager not to lose contact with him again. '*And, of course, your own.*'

'It was him, captain.'

'*Who, sergeant?*'

'Kurtha Sedd…'

There's a pause, before the captain enquires on.

'*Are you injured?*' Aethon presses. '*Has your squad sustained casualties?*'

'My squad,' Dardanus begins. 'They're… They're all dead.'

'*Are you injured, sergeant?*'

Dardanus looks down at his belly and the innards spilling out of it. A feeble smile of hopelessness briefly cracks the stricken mask of his face.

'Are you inj…' Dardanus fades.

'*Sergeant?*'

'Yes. I'm injured.'

'*Sergeant!*' the captain barks. '*Listen to me. Status? Describe your injuries. Are you combat capable?*'

'No,' Dardanus hisses through gritted teeth. 'Sustained a laceration from the omphalic, out through the external oblique and latissimus dorsi. Plate breached. Carapace breached.

Oolitics and viscera ruptured.' For a moment, Dardanus's composure breaks. 'I'm spilling blood and guts all over the place.'

'*Are there hostiles nearby?*' Aethon asks.

'I don't know,' Dardanus answers, desperate to cling on to consciousness. 'I don't think so.'

'*Don't move,*' the captain orders. '*We're coming to you, brother. Where are you?*'

'I don't know,' Dardanus answers honestly.

'*Think, sergeant.*'

'I don't know,' the Ultramarine returns with feeble anger.

'*Describe your surroundings.*' A new voice: Sergeant Urcus, his words tinged with an uncommon concern.

Dardanus looks about him. 'A tunnel.'

'*Any distinguishing markings?*' Urcus asks. '*Glyphs? Signs?*'

'Nothing...' Dardanus croaks, lowering his head.

'*Stay with me, brother,*' Aethon says. '*We're coming to get you.*'

'Lost... a lot of... blood...' Dardanus mumbles, his attention straying.

'*Sergeant Dardanus,*' Aethon says. '*Report. Are the walls rough or smooth?*'

'Smooth...'

Dardanus can hear the captain and Sergeant Urcus talking. It sounds as though they are hurriedly consulting over a map.

'*He must be in the sub-levels. What about the Conduis Lacrimae?*'

'*That's off the squad's route. More likely the Tantum Infinita or one of the arterial offshoots. The Nullius or the Testari.*'

Arkan Dardanus feels the darkness taking him.

'*Dardanus?*'

He cannot speak.

'Sergeant, answer me.'

'Captain...' Dardanus hisses down the vox.

'I'm coming for you myself,' Aethon tells him. *'Do you hear me, brother?'*

Through the blood and the darkness, Dardanus feels the approach of death. Behind his pain-scrunched eyes, he can still see the ghoulish green blaze of the Chaplain's eye-lenses. It is as though Kurtha Sedd is with him, come to feast on the misery of his last moments. In his imagination, the Chaplain is more terrifying than ever.

'Kurtha Sedd...' Dardanus says, his words weak and removed, as if uttered in the tumult of a nightmare.

'Dardanus, try not to...'

'Listen,' Dardanus says. 'Can you hear him?'

'Hear who, brother?'

'The Chaplain has a message for you...'

For a moment, the vox is silent and then Aethon returns, his voice hollow with fury and woe. *'You are that message. I asked and Kurtha Sedd answered.'*

'He wants you to go to him,' Dardanus coughs and splutters.

'Yes.'

'A trap, captain.'

'Yes, brother.'

'You will kill him?' Dardanus manages, feeling his chest rise and fall for the last time.

'For you, brother,' Aethon promises, his words dark and driven. *'For all our brothers.'*

With the captain's oath echoing through his helm, Arkan Dardanus dies. Blood glistens about him in a thick puddle. The darkness smothers him like a living entity. Throughout the tunnel, all that can be heard is the roar of the helm vox. An Ultramarines captain calling out his battle-brother's name. The words harsh, hoarse and furious.

TEN

[mark: 139.21.54]

WHILE THE SURFACE of Calth rages in the immolating fires of the Veridian star, the depths of the underworld shake with the fury of Steloc Aethon of the Honoured 19th, whose company has been smashed in the unfolding atrocity of the Word Bearers attack. Aethon, who has held out a gauntlet to a man he had called friend, with the promise of a nobility restored, only to find the blood of innocent Ultramarines on his hands. Aethon the White Spider – who has ventured into the depths many times before in search of predatory foes.

The time has come. The stellar storm has driven Ultramarines and Word Bearers alike into the shelter of the arcologies. This underworld – all that is now left of mighty Calth – is still part of Ultramar, still a part of the Emperor's Imperium. The traitor and the deviant have tainted it with their presence long enough. Aethon will no longer play at tactics and territory in the dark. There will be no war in the shadows, no monsters like Kurtha Sedd and his fallen kindred to fight. Aethon will forge on into the depths. He will force the Word Bearers back and back until they burn in the cleansing fires of the planetary core, and Calth finally has its revenge.

Aethon sends for *Moricorpus* and summons his sergeants. The combi-weapon has been cleaned, polished and replenished with ammunition. With noble legionaries of all companies at his side and Squad Daedal leading the charge of the Honoured 19th, the Ultramarines have punched through the gathering ranks of Word Bearers once more laying siege to the command tower. Power-armoured legionaries and Cataphractii Terminators all working together, like the finely crafted pieces of a well-oiled machine.

While Sergeant Urcus and his assigned squads hold the rearguard, protecting the Ultramarines force and the teleportarium from Word Bearers following them, Aethon pushes on. The captain is a brutal force of nature – the legionary equivalent of a meteorite blasting into the side of a planet, or a hurricane tearing across the surface of a gas giant.

Something has filled their captain with a grim, unrelenting wrath, and the Ultramarines know it. Aethon moves from chamber to cavern, tunnel to intersection, *Moricorpus* spitting death into charging Word Bearers. His chainfist tears through enemies, lopping off heads and limbs, carving through plate, carapace and ribcages. His advance is unstoppable, outpacing his rearguard. The force has become spread along the route, moving through collapsing arcology sections and the corpses of fallen Word Bearers. Aethon's face is fixed in a grim visage of barely repressed rage. Orders are issued through the pugnacity of a snarl, while his tactics are bold and fearless.

His sergeants answer the call, the Ultramarines finally let off the leash to fight an aggressor's war. Without territories to maintain and strategic outposts to defend, the sons of Guilliman can channel their own loss, grief and fury into attack patterns of devastating force and precision.

It is exactly what the Word Bearers don't expect.

Arriving in consolidated number to lay siege to Captain Aethon and his command tower, they had planned to overwhelm the Ultramarines. Their surprise attack suddenly turned into Aethon's own, with the captain throwing nearly every Ultramarine he had in aggressive tactical formations at just one section of the enemy cordon. With the command nexus collapsing about them, Aethon leads through the darkness, through the enemy and into the depths.

'Advance, and lay down covering fire,' he orders into his suit vox. 'Sergeant Daedal – with me.'

He leaves the cover of a pillar and stomps forwards, cutting down a Word Bearer with *Moricorpus*'s boltgun. The sub-arcology chamber is situated on the border of the Tantum Infinita and the rocky underworld of the cavernous sub-levels. Beyond lie the depths that Kurtha Sedd's fiends have fled to and made their own. Blanketed in a thick, unnatural darkness that cannot be pierced by the eye, optic filter or auspex, the fighting in the undervault is close and bloody.

A missile shrieks out from a gloom-cloaked corner, searing between the pillars at Aethon's crossing. Interrupting his advance, the captain slows his armoured momentum, allowing the missile to flash before his breastplate. Sending a hail of bolt-rounds into the corner, Aethon reaches the shadow of another pillar.

'Squad Sarpedus, move up to support the vanguard!' he roars. 'Phineon – by twos to the choke point. I want that gauntlet broken!'

He doesn't wait for Daedal and his Terminators. By the time the sergeant is there, power fist against the bolt-shredded column and his own weapon tearing apart Word Bearers, the captain is off again. Cutting through the helm of a flanking foe with the spinning blur of his chainblade, Aethon turns with his combi-weapon raised once more. The two traitors that follow are enveloped in a succession of shimmering blasts from the captain's melta.

And yet *still* they come, legionary madmen who charge at the Terminator captain with little more than pistols and chainswords, and blind, furious faith.

'Pattern Extempio, brothers! Extempio!' Aethon berates as he slaughters his way through the lesser warriors of the XVII Legion. As the Ultramarines nearby take their correction, the captain drives his fist into the scripture-adorned helm of a Word Bearer, knocking it into the skull of the warrior behind. Gunning the chainblade, Aethon cleaves the heads from both warriors with a single, slashing stroke.

'Autolo, Lycastus – watch your corners,' the captain barks. 'I want that flank, damn it!'

As Aethon bats aside a chainsword, all but demolishing the lesser weapon, another missile streaks from the gloom and showers him with shattered masonry from a large, square pillar at his back. The chamber shakes, and hewn stone rains from its upper reaches.

'Sergeant Idas,' the captain calls across the vox. 'Would it be too much to ask you to neutralise that launcher?'

With Idas and his power-armoured legionaries moving on the chamber corner, Aethon thuds a stream of bolts into the Word Bearer clutching the wrecked chainsword. As his foe staggers back, Aethon stamps an armoured boot into the traitor's midriff, breaking him almost in two.

'Forward the heavy flamers,' Aethon commands. 'Burn out that side chamber, enemy and all.'

Terminators advance with promethium dribbling from the barrels of their heavy weapons, but an almighty crack spreads across the ceiling of the undervault ahead of them, weaving its way through the pillars and into the side chamber. Weakened by numerous impact detonations, the vault suddenly gives way, setting in motion a chain reaction of collapses with chambers falling through those beneath.

The Terminators and their supporting squad disappear in an avalanche of masonry, a dusty cloud billowing its way through the thick darkness. The side chamber and the Word Bearers within are gone, pulverised by the cascade of rock. The dust is followed by flames that gutter and stream from an open fissure overhead – a venting torrent feeling its way down through the levels from the stellar storm above.

Thrusting his combi-weapon at Word Bearers coming at him from the murk and miasma, Aethon guns them down before they can regroup. He joins Squad Lantor who are attempting to dig the buried Terminators out, using the power in his Tactical Dreadnought suit to heave and roll massive chunks of stone from the settled mound. Bolt-rounds pluck at his plate and sparks dance from the thick armour. Moving a huge boulder from the crushed body of an Ultramarines legionary, Aethon feels the burn of his previous wound radiate out from his side. The plasma shot he suffered during the surface battle pains him still, forcing him to drop the boulder and clutch at the damaged plate.

'Get them out,' Aethon grunts at Sergeant Lantor. He can still see the outstretched gauntlets of Ultramarines Terminators reaching from the collapse. Withering fire from the chamber exit hammers into the captain, almost knocking him off-balance. 'Pyramon! Take your squad and give me a counter-clockwise rotation on that exit. Keep the front ranks under pressure. Daedal and I will break it wide open.'

'Aye, brother-captain,' Pyramon returns, but Aethon barely hears him.

The captain is walking straight into the enemy bolter fire. With Daedal and his squad of Terminators fanning out behind, their combi-bolters thundering back at the Word Bearers, Aethon presents himself at the spearhead of the assault.

The sheer force of bolt-rounds thudding off his plate steals the air from his lungs, but he will not be denied. Onwards. Ever onwards.

Beyond the Word Bearers is a blast door. Beyond that are the depths.

Hiding there, like some lowly creature that creeps or crawls, is Kurtha Sedd.

Aethon will not stop until he has the Chaplain in his sights. No ambush will slow his progress. No legionary will stand in his way. No blade or bolt-round will put him from his destiny – a destiny in which the Chaplain will pay not only for his part in his Legion's treachery but for his personal failure to see reason, to see the hand of former comradeship in Aethon's actions and the chance to regain at least a little of his honour.

As the Word Bearers at the door are forced to split their fire between Aethon and Pyramon's squad, the captain breaks into a heavy run. Stone fractures beneath his footsteps and the mountain of plate about him groans with the rhythm of it. Aethon can hear Daedal and his squad keeping pace. As traitors come out firing from behind pillars or slicing through the unnatural gloom with chainswords, Aethon and the Terminators drop them with economic bursts of mass-reactives.

Some blindly aim their bucking boltguns from the cover of a felled stone pillar. Those that stand to offer themselves in combat are riddled with bolter fire from Pyramon's legionaries and closing squads under Sergeants Sarpedus and Phineon.

Aethon slows before putting one mighty, armoured foot upon the pillar and rolling it back into the Word Bearers. Flushed out, desperate enemy troops launch themselves forwards. It does them little good: the Ultramarines are a closing wall of ceramite and certainty, through which nothing will pass. Sergeant Daedal knocks one of them senseless to the floor with a downward thump of his power fist, while others are torn back in a furious confluence of bolter fire.

A legionary bearing a pair of smoke-trailing daggers comes at Aethon like an assassin, but one of Daedal's Terminators blasts him clear of the captain's path. As the firefight dies down and the background rumble of distant quakes returns, Aethon finds the last of the Word Bearers hammering on the blast door with his fist. It is sealed, but the traitors behind the door will not open it for their compatriot. The Word Bearer turns in panic, his back to the door.

Aethon raises *Moricorpus*. The warrior drops his empty boltgun.

'I am loyal to the Emper–' he begins, but Aethon does not let him finish.

The captain unleashes a staccato hail of bolt-rounds into the legionary, emptying the clip. Before the Word Bearer has even dropped to the ground against the door, Aethon is there, laying a gauntlet on the metal and putting his ear to its surface.

'Reload,' he calls out, prompting Sergeant Idas to despatch an Ultramarine to take *Moricorpus* and exchange both its bolt magazine and melta reserve. 'Squads, form up.'

This is what their bloody progress has been – fighting Word Bearers along the lengths of tunnels and passageways before mounting more determined actions to take the larger chambers and caverns. Beyond the blast door lies another passageway and yet more Word Bearers through which Aethon's rotating squads and formations will punch.

From behind the door, Aethon hears a sharp crack and a *whoosh*. It is a sound that he recognises. The crackling energies of immaterial transference feeling their way through the metal of the door confirm what his sensors are telling him.

'Teleport signature. Take position on the door.' He switches channels on the vox. 'Sergeant Urcus – I'm afraid you missed the best part of the action, old friend…'

As the blast door begins to judder upwards, Ultramarines assume cover and overlapping fire arcs on the chamber exit. Aethon backs up and finds *Moricorpus* thrust back into his waiting grip, and he readies himself to receive much-needed reinforcements from their rearguard.

The darkness is thick behind the door, threaded through with the lead-coloured smoke of translation. As it clears, Aethon is surprised to see nothing there. Beyond the door the Word Bearers have set up teleporter nodes of their own, equipment stripped out of a bulk cargo facility like the one at the Proprium-Termini. They have jury-rigged the equipment in the broad passage as a homer for a rough local translation.

Aethon realises that the Word Bearer he has just killed wasn't trying to get through the door. He was signalling his compatriots, but the gambit has not paid off. Through the gloom and the crackling of residual energies across the stone walls, the captain can see retreating Word Bearers, armoured troops falling back after the failure of the translation.

As the Ultramarines hold, their weapons trained on the exit, Aethon allows himself some grim satisfaction. Hopefully, the Word Bearers reinforcements have teleported into solid rock.

'Onwards,' he announces, his voice full of hollow fury.

Recovering ammunition and fresh weapons from the fallen, the Ultramarines pause when they see that their captain has stopped only a short way ahead.

Aethon stands over a body: an Ultramarine who had been crawling up the passage on his belly. The plate and cabling at his side betray a grievous wound where some weapon has sawed through his torso. The warrior has suffered further desecration where marching Word Bearers have stamped the cadaver into the ground as they passed.

The captain stands in the pool of blood surrounding the legionary, looking at the trail of red left in his wake as he dragged himself through the labyrinthine underworld. Blood, entrails, gore, all leading back to where the Ultramarine was assaulted.

Back to where Arkan Dardanus's fate was sealed.

That was where Aethon would find Kurtha Sedd.

'Return to Macragge, son of Guilliman,' Aethon murmurs, his lips stinging with the bitterness of the words. 'Walk the Gardens of Locastra. Climb Gallan's Rock and know that, like the rebel consul himself, all traitors are punished. We shall be that instrument of punishment here and, like the rock, we shall remain unmoved and unbroken. Find peace in the plunging falls of Hera's Crown and watch the sunset over the fortress of our father – for your fight is over, legionary. The primarch and his Emperor have asked all they can of you. Wait for me there, about the temples, halls and monuments – for one day we all must follow where you lead, brother.'

He offers a solemn salute, knowing that the others with him do the same.

'Come,' he says finally to the Ultramarines at his back.

'Our enemy awaits, and Sergeant Dardanus has shown us the way.'

ELEVEN

[mark: 140.48.33]

STONE RUMBLES ASIDE. Dust erupts in a cloud of disturbance, and Aethon climbs through the opening. One passage blurs into another, all the collapsed caverns and benighted chambers in the rocky bowels of the planet. It has been like this for leagues. The captain stands in his Terminator suit, his ceramite fingertips now tools for prising open demolished entrances and his fists two hammers with which to batter aside the masonry blocking their way.

All about the Ultramarines, the thunder of moving rock can be heard. The pulverising crunch of stone. The creak and split of fissures opening above and around them. The boom of star-ravaged buildings tumbling, falling and crashing down through their own foundations. The quakes and shockwaves feeling their way down through vaults, arcologies and sub-levels, shaking the underworld of Calth all the way to the core. Everything moves. Everything shakes and quivers. Grit pours down through openings in plumes of rock dust and, when it doesn't, raging cascades of flame blast down through the ruins of the shattered network.

The command tower and its surrounding arcology are behind them. With it Aethon has left the corpses of the Word Bearers so desperate to claim it for their dread masters. Only the depths remain. He leads the sons of Guilliman through the subterranean death trap, guided by the blood trail and his right hand, Brother Medon, who has spent more time hunched over a runebank studying the system maps than all his battle-brothers put together.

There have been losses, but Aethon leads the Ultramarines through the quaking subterranean maze of collapses and flaming torrents regardless. As it has always been, the dead will be honoured in the fullness of time.

'Stop,' he commands, bringing the Ultramarines to a standstill.

Between the quakes they hear it. A sound torturously contorted by the derelict labyrinth and ordinarily lost in the booming thunder from above.

'Is that... chanting?'

Sergeant Phineon listens. It is distant and all but lost in the echoing rumbles that shake the bones of Calth, but it is there. The longer they listen, the more the foul words and unspeakable rhythms worm their way into the mind. They claw at sanity and fill the heart with dread.

'It must be the Urizen's spawn,' Phineon spits. 'I've seen some strange things fighting those mongrels, both on the surface and in the depths. They are lost to some dark worship – ceremonies and superstitions unbecoming a legionary of the Emperor.'

Aethon answers with a nod.

The Ultramarines move on at speed through the twists and crooks of the passageway, following the trail of gore. In some areas the architecture has been shattered by movements in the rock above or blocked by venting flame. Working through the surrounding fractures and squeezing their plate through gaps into newly revealed chambers, the Ultramarines pick up the smeared trail again each time. As they do so, they marvel. Arkan Dardanus has dragged his injured body for an unimaginable distance up out of the rocky sub-levels. The Ultramarines try not to imagine the pain and horror that their fellow legionary must have suffered.

As the way ahead becomes dominated once more by tumbling stone and raging flame, the blood trail takes a torturous turn and ends in a disembowelling slash of red. Aethon takes a sharp breath, seeing the bodies of Squad Sephirus lying in the dust nearby.

The Ultramarines move on, the cloying gloom growing thicker and the chanting ever more pervasive. Aethon feels sick at the sound of repeated incantations and sharp Colchisian syllables. He can hear the bitterness and hatred in the haunted voices as they wrap their tongues around the unnatural words. He tries to repeat one half-heard phrase under his breath, but the syllables taste sour on his palate.

His power-armoured Ultramarines fan out around him, their boltguns tucked in tightly to their shoulders, establishing a perimeter at the edge of the new cavern beyond. Aethon has no memory of anything like this. It is a raw and crooked place of eternal darkness that was never meant to see the light.

Beyond the tumbled masonry and the great pillars that divide the space, there is movement.

It is the Word Bearers, and a handful of their degenerate mortal followers.

Beyond them, there is only black. It is the starless expanse of the extra-galactic void, multiplied back upon itself a hundred times over and filled to the brim with unspeakable, eternal malevolence. The chanting traitors are gathered on the edge of a great abyss that descends far deeper than the unaided eye can see.

His need for vengeance rising within him, Aethon signals his warriors to form up. He stoops behind some hastily erected traitor barricade of scrap iron to check his ammunition gauges, then guns the motors of his chainfist.

'Brothers, destroy the dishonoured!' he roars, cleaving through the barricade. 'Now!'

The sons of Guilliman answer. Fury and surprise combine with their tactical training, and the cacophony of gunfire echoes into the darkness. Splitting into two contingents, squads of Ultramarines move along the irregularity of the cavern walls, the blue of their plate faded with drifting dust. Their movements are bold. They are brave and indomitable, moving from crook to crevice, boulder to outcrop. Boltguns thud with concentrated streams of merciless gunfire. Precious grenades bounce through the shadows, turning the murk into the brightness of blossoming detonation and flailing bodies.

Legionaries fall on both sides, the savage return fire of the Word Bearers finding its mark with equal accuracy. But there is no stopping. Aethon will not–

A powerful roar reverberates through the air, and *something* lumbers into the cavern.

The armoured machine is covered in brain-aching sigils and glowing scripture. As it shakes debris from its legs and heavy weaponry, the captain makes out the unmistakable silhouette of a Contemptor Dreadnought. It stamps forth with another inhuman, static-laced roar.

'Destroy it!' the captain roars, as if his Ultramarines needed any such prompting.

Bolter fire showers the heavily armoured Dreadnought but it stalks forwards, smashing its clenched power fist into the rough wall for stability while bringing a damaged assault cannon online. A cone of fire flashes before the rotary weapon as the barrels unleash a shredding stream of shells into the Ultramarines' position.

Aethon turns side-on as the storm engulfs him, like a hundred hammerblows ricocheting from his armour. He staggers, the concentrated fire of the Dreadnought tearing up his breastplate and finding the joints beneath his curved pauldron. Tiny pieces of shredded ceramite sting the flesh of the captain's face, while a round cuts at his jaw and a second skins his temple. The underworld suddenly tumbles away as Aethon falls back over a mound of debris.

'Protect the captain!' Sergeant Phineon roars, launching himself out into the open.

'Hold position,' Aethon manages to call out above the roar of the assault cannon, but it is too late. Legionaries from Phineon's squad break from cover to blast the Dreadnought with krak missiles and instantly become blurs of gore and shredded plate, Phineon included.

The Contemptor appears driven on by some dark force. Its corrupted auto-senses guide its deadly weaponry while the silky darkness of the passage streams about the Dreadnought like a great cloak.

As Aethon's vox-link crackles in and out, he is only half aware of the carnage erupting about him. The Dreadnought fights like a thing possessed, venturing forth to soak up the precision fire of the Ultramarines with its sigil-scorched plate. It methodically rips through cover and then the legionaries with its assault cannon, crazed and ragged human auxiliaries following in its wake.

As Terminators from Squad Daedal attempt to close with the thing, the Contemptor unleashes another furious attack with its sizzling fist. It punches Ultramarines through columns and into the rendered stone of the walls, then grabs at Pheroneus Daedal's helm and crushes the sergeant's head within a vice of monstrous digits.

Aethon hauls the bulk of his Cataphractii suit back to its feet. The armour is unwieldy and all but impossible to right without help, but the captain manages it. With Ultramarines dying all around, he rises once more from behind the fallen debris.

'No...' the captain growls as he stomps towards the berserk Dreadnought. The machine is so invested in its slaughter that it barely notices Aethon's approach. 'Break it open!' the honoured captain of the 19th bellows, and breaks into a slow run. 'Kill the accursed thing!'

Keying into the approaching threat, the Contemptor turns its cannon towards Aethon, but the captain hammers the sparking barrels aside with his chainfist. Ramming into the Dreadnought, Aethon hits it in the chest with his armoured forearms like a pugilist forcing back a crowding opponent.

The Dreadnought staggers back with the impact, gifting the

Ultramarines a precious second's advantage. Melta charges are primed, clamped to the beast's armoured frame even as it lashes out at the closest legionaries.

The twin blasts sear through adamantium plate, melting armour with the focused heat of a new sun. It is enough to rival even the wrath of Veridia.

In a shower of sparks the wounded Word Bearers Dreadnought stumbles to the floor. One of the monstrous machine's legs buckles beneath its own jarred mechanism, and it howls in mechanical agony. Yet still the cursed thing resists, attempting to drag itself back up on overstrained piston-muscles, its weapons firing wildly, sigils burning even brighter in the swirling darkness.

Aethon plunges his chainfist into the breach. The knuckles of his gauntlet strike shredded plate and he glares into the flickering eye-lenses of the struggling machine.

All he sees there is immortal, unyielding madness. The insanity of the foetid Word Bearers champion enshrined within.

He roars. The Dreadnought roars back.

It bats him aside, shredding a handful of scrambling humans and legionaries with a final sweep of cannon-fire. The captain's chainfist tears out of the thing in a fountain of blood, oil and internment fluid as Aethon tumbles away, sending the Contemptor into a wild, berserk spin. The sigils flare and fade. Its reactor begins to die. The molten edges of its plate spatter the rocky floor with liquefied plasteel.

It howls again, and sweeps up a dozen friends and foes in its blinded, flailing path, straight into a great stone column. It manages three more broken steps before it topples forwards, crashing down and over the edge of the precipice in a grinding tumble of heavy, iron limbs.

Aethon stands. What remains of his Ultramarines stand also, emerging from cover and the carnage. They might cheer the thing's destruction, were it not for the many foes that still remain. Moving past his fallen brothers, the captain leads his men forwards. Closing on the Word Bearers gathered at the precipice, Aethon storms through the hail of bolt-rounds, thrusting *Moricorpus* at Word Bearer after Word Bearer, blasting enemies from his path. He turns the traitors to molten slag with streams of sub-atomic heat and cuts down any that survive with savage arcs of his chainfist.

He barks orders across the vox, encouraging his squads to take advantage of openings and new positions. All the while his hearts pump with bitter rage. His face is screwed up with the desire to avenge, to kill and to win. He despatches lesser legionaries with purpose and cold savagery.

The Word Bearers spread out, and the Ultramarines with them. Formations disintegrate. The fighting becomes close. The darkness is a melee of clashing plate, gunfire and death. A missile takes an Ultramarine from Aethon's side, blasting him bodily from his feet in a spray of gory shrapnel.

'Strike hard, brothers!' the captain urges, blinking the red from his eyes. 'Strike–'

He feels a sudden, icy pressure building in the base of his skull, and a flash of blue casts harsh shadows on the rocky walls of the cavern. Orestrian Urcus, his armour trailing arcs of frozen teleportation energy, leads his Cataphractii into the fray in a great, lumbering counter-charge. The reinforcements have arrived.

Aethon whirls around, taking the head from another crimson-armoured traitor. He stares down into the chasm, an abyss reaching into the depths of Calth. From it, the seemingly sentient gloom rises like a black cloud, spreading into the underworld beyond.

'Nineteenth – right pincer,' Aethon roars to his sergeants and brothers. 'Drive them in! Let them taste of oblivion!'

He strides towards the ritual circle, and his warriors send two Word Bearers staggering backwards over the precipice with cries that ring out far longer than they have any logical right to. Aethon allows himself a bitter laugh of satisfaction, and turns to–

His hearts stop.

Not ten metres in front of him stands a Word Bearers Chaplain, in a crested helm and tattered cloak. His scriptured plate appears to smoulder in the gloom.

Kurtha Sedd.

Kurtha Sedd.

Kurtha Sedd!

He gestures to the stunned Aethon with his crozius – the very weapon that saved the Ultramarine's life on Melior-Tertia. His words come through the vox-grille of his grimy helm with an unholy clarity.

'Steloc, the truth of Chaos is all around us,' he calls out. 'Surrender to it!'

The captain is the cold fire of his primarch's wrath. Expert, assured, deadly. Aethon walks towards the Chaplain. His steps are righteous, his weapons ready. He has his old friend – nay, his new enemy – cornered. The fury of the battle about them seems to fade into the distance. There is only Steloc Aethon and Kurtha Sedd.

The Chaplain flicks his cloak to one side. He holds his crozius and plasma pistol at his sides, stepping carefully into the shadow of a great pillar. 'The Octed is strong here. The flames of darkness shall consume you all!'

Fury blazes white-hot in Aethon's mind. All rational thought is driven from him.

'Shut up, traitor!' he bellows, hurling himself forwards.

Kurtha Sedd's plasma pistol snaps up and unleashes a searing shot, but Aethon sidesteps it without conscious thought and slashes out with his chainfist. The Word Bearer spins to one side, using the advantage of his lighter armour to outpace Aethon's charge, and the chainfist chews into the pillar instead in a spray of rock dust.

'There will be no surrender,' the captain snarls. 'For either of us. You had your chance for an honourable death.'

The two genhanced warriors clash, throwing everything they have at one another in an explosion of blistering hatred. Kurtha Sedd brings his crozius around in a brutal arc and smashes *Moricorpus* to pieces. Aethon dodges the blazing orb of another plasma blast to swing his chainblade around with merciless force. The ferocious battle unfolds like doom finding its form.

Steloc Aethon and Kurtha Sedd.

Captain and Chaplain.

Ultramarine and Word Bearer.

Friend and foe.

Aethon's chainfist roars and tears the plasma pistol straight out of the Chaplain's jarred gauntlet. His movements are practised, sure-footed – the epitome of the primarch's codified excellence and the pinnacle of XIII Legion training, only now edged with disbelief, betrayal and outrage. By contrast, Kurtha Sedd carries his manoeuvres with the flair of maniacal invulnerability. His sweeps and strikes are those of a man who believes that he simply cannot lose.

Aethon swings with the fury of Guilliman, a rage that is channelled to enhance rather than unbalance the execution of martial superiority. He blocks his opponent from slipping past, keeping the Chaplain between himself and the yawning blackness beyond.

The pair weave and spar on the edge of the abyss. To a worthy remembrancer, it might be a spectacle of miserable beauty. Warriors at the height of their prowess, fighting to destroy – or perhaps to save? – one another.

They begin to slow. Not from fatigue, but from the dread realisation that there might be *another* way. Aethon grits his teeth. In spite of everything he has witnessed and everything he has done… all of the horror, the carnage and the bloodshed… there *is* another way.

He tries to find the words, but Kurtha Sedd brings the crozius around in a powerful arc, catching him on the shoulder with a flare of powered force.

Aethon stumbles at the lip of the chasm, feeling the rock give way beneath his heavily armoured feet. Cracks spread. He reels back, throwing his weight away from the edge as rubble tumbles into the darkness below. For the longest moment, he teeters on the brink. Then he takes a solid step back, bringing his chainfist around in a defensive stance.

Kurtha Sedd holds an ornate sacrificial dagger in his other hand.

It is already inside Aethon's guard, beneath his outstretched arm.

The instant stretches out into an eternity. The dagger glints cruelly before his eyes.

The Chaplain steps in close, taking Aethon in a brotherly

embrace. The blade slips through the seals beneath his pauldron, plunging deep between the Ultramarine's ribs.

There is no pain. No contorted expression of rage. Aethon's face is a mask of empty disbelief, his eyes dark pinpoints of hopelessness and betrayal. He takes several short, gasping breaths. An icy cold spreads from the killing wound.

Kurtha Sedd brings his faceplate in close to Aethon's ear, but his words are as distant and indistinct as the infernal whispers that now rise from the abyss.

TWELVE

[mark: 141.02.01]

URCUS WATCHES THE knife go in – into his captain, into his friend. A shudder of shock passes through the sergeant. The moment feels unreal and yet, as the blade slides between ceramite plates and into Aethon's flesh, it is almost as though the knife has entered his own.

Kurtha Sedd holds the captain, his blade all the way home, skewering Aethon on the lip of the precipice.

The abyss beckons. Urcus feels himself drawn into the smothering darkness and the chaos of battle unending. The desperation of legionaries fighting not only for the ideals of a fallen Imperium but for their very lives. Enemies to vanquish. Friends and brothers to save. Urcus holds on to the seconds as Kurtha Sedd holds on to his captain. The sergeant can't let this happen. There must be another way. If only he had arrived sooner; if only he had not let the vanguard of the force outpace them so dramatically.

But self-recrimination fades with the urgency of the moment. There is no time for blame. Only action. With his lightning claws ready, the sergeant lumbers forwards. Destiny – or some dark thing like it – draws him on, his shattered plate rattling about him.

All around, like phantoms in the gloom, legionaries of the XIII and XVII Legions fight to the death on the edge of the chasm. Swords clash, chainblades spark and the fire of bolt-guns rips through power-armoured bodies and into bare rock. Warriors try to tear each other from their purchase to stamp and throttle the life out of one another. Knives flash in the darkness and lifeless bodies tumble down into the bowels of the planet. Rocks and grit rain from above with each fresh quake radiating from the surface, dusting the armour of friend and foe alike and rendering them as phantoms in the murk.

All the while the Word Bearers maintain their chant, their incantations hailing from their grilles in glorious unison. The sickening words and sounds have become a frenzied battle cry, echoing from the vaulted cavern above and the seemingly bottomless abyss extending below.

And at the heart of it all stands Kurtha Sedd.

Kurtha Sedd the traitor. The would-be slayer of heroes.

Urcus's focus is shattered as a crazed Word Bearer leaps down from an outcrop above, landing on the sergeant's armoured carapace. Snarling, Urcus crashes the back of his plate, attacker and all, into a rocky outcrop – as the Word Bearer falls, another hurls himself in with a boltgun stretched out before him. Urcus swings with his bladed fist, smashing the weapon out of the traitor's hand; then, bringing the claw back, he guts him, ripping his entrails out before whirling him around and over the precipice.

Other crimson-clad bodies fall, forcing Urcus to lean this way and that to avoid them. He can hear Ultramarines gunfire driving the Word Bearers back. With so many enemy targets, the din is relentless.

A dead weight crashes into him, toppling him sideways. In desperation, Urcus drives his right claw into the crumbling rock at the very edge of the chasm just as his heavily armoured legs kick out into nothingness.

His stomach lurches. The cold darkness beckons.

He cannot get an angle to pierce the rock with his other claw, and his gauntleted fingers scratch for any handhold he can manage.

Struggling to regain his purchase and with the heavy Cataphractii suit dragging him down like an anchor, Urcus peers up. He finds a Word Bearer on the ledge above him, the ledge he is holding on to.

It is not just any traitor. Urcus recognises the plate markings of one of the prisoners from the command tower. Without his helm, the warrior glowers down at him from behind a bolt pistol. He gives the sergeant a wicked smile and cocks the weapon.

Urcus growls in frustration and rips his claw out of the ledge, tearing the Word Bearer's foothold away. The traitor pitches forwards, his face a stricken mask, screaming into the void as he falls to his timely death.

Urcus's Cataphractii suit has become a ceramite coffin about the sergeant, threatening to drag him down into the abyss. The honoured plate has given everything it has. Gripping as tightly as he can with both gauntlets, Orestrian Urcus simply hangs there, holding on for his very existence.

His teeth gritted, he glances sideways at Kurtha Sedd, who still clings tightly to the shuddering form of Captain Aethon. The Chaplain is whispering something to him.

Then, with a terrible and final silence, Kurtha Sedd pushes Aethon away, allowing the captain to stumble back off the cruel-looking blade. The Ultramarine totters, then falls back off the edge of the rocky precipice.

Urcus cannot even form words and instead roars his disbelief. The shock gives him the renewed strength to haul his armoured chest up onto the ledge. He heaves the entire suit up with the raw power in his exhausted arms, dragging himself onto one knee with his lightning claws ready.

As he does so, Kurtha Sedd turns.

The legionaries stare at one another.

The chanting has stopped. Something is happening.

A deep rumble, far more ominous than any warquake in the underworld of Calth, builds in the depths. The darkness clings to Kurtha Sedd like a second skin, as if in celebration of his grim efforts. Ghostly fire flickers on the edges of perception.

Orestrian Urcus narrows his eyes. 'There isn't anywhere you can go on this planet where we won't find you, traitor,' he spits at the Chaplain.

Kurtha Sedd, who could easily fracture the ledge with a single blow from his crozius or barge the sergeant back into the abyss, seems unsure of himself – dazed, almost. He pauses before a ravaged stone column.

'There isn't anywhere on this planet *to* go,' the Chaplain replies before melting away into purest darkness.

Urcus rises. The rock beneath his feet is trembling.

He hears someone shouting his name. He recognises the voice. Brother Medon.

'Urcus! Get out of there!'

Breaking into a lumbering run, the sergeant looks around him. The Word Bearers have not broken from combat, but they are moving away from the chasm. What could cause such vile traitors to turn tail and run? Urcus stares down into the depths – down into the black heart of the planet.

What he sees all but defies description.

The darkness has given birth to horrors.

Monstrosities of every shape and form, creatures of nightmare and stomach-churning whimsy. Things not human, things without even a xenos uniformity. Things of fear made flesh, climbing, crawling, slithering and stalking up the walls of the chasm. Unspeakable beings brought forth only half-crafted from some benighted place by Kurtha Sedd, to feast upon loyal warriors of the Legiones Astartes.

The Word Bearers are exultant. He hears a cry go up from elsewhere in the chamber. He cannot tell if it comes from a rational mind rejecting the insanity of what it sees, or from the maniacal zealotry of old superstitions.

'Daemons! Daemons!' it howls.

Daemons.

Urcus grimaces. Every movement is an effort in the mountain of dying armour. His leg will not bear his weight. Hobbling backwards, he keeps his claws outstretched. The servos and fibre bundles of the Cataphractii suit seem to resist his every movement, but by will alone the sergeant forces the suit into action.

Otherworldly creatures of freakish dread surround him, slithering across the back wall and curling their horrific bodies about the rock of the precipice. Things of daggered tooth and razored maw hiss their intention to swallow his soul. Perversities of horn, pincer and claw chitter and shriek. Tails swish suggestively and flick with dripping barbs, while inhuman forms with too many arms and legs crawl forth from the abyss.

Orestrian Urcus has never seen their like before. He hopes never to again.

If he survives.

All along the edge of the chasm, beasts of the beyond skitter up the rock face to set upon escaping Ultramarines and Word Bearers alike. Creatures erupt with tentacular appendages that drag legionaries down. Others vomit acidic juices up at them, catching falling warriors in enveloping wings that muffle their victims' screams, stabbing noble Space Marines through the back before plucking them from their footing and into the abyss.

'Come on then, you abominations,' Urcus tells the nightmare visions closing in about him. 'Too polite to come and get me? Let me make it easy for you.'

He lifts one of his metal claws with arm-breaking effort, ready to cut down a fiendish beast that has stalked in closer than the rest of the pack. He knows that this will be the end of their short-lived war in the underworld.

He is, therefore, surprised when the creature's head explodes, spattering warped brains and ichor all over his suit. The other disgusting monstrosities about him howl and shriek with explosive death as their bodies, heads and appendages are shredded by bolter fire. Others die on the chasm wall, tumbling back into the depths.

Looking back, Urcus sees battle-fresh Ultramarines spreading out around the edge of the abyss with Brother Medon, helping wounded brother legionaries to their feet and laying down a merciless hail of suppressing fire. Rather than face the guns of their foes, some desperate Word Bearers even hurl themselves into the abyss after their *daemon* creatures.

As the legionary reinforcements take position throughout the chamber, heavy bolters and missile launchers are expertly deployed. The support weapons chew into the more resilient beasts that boast foetid bulk, chitinous shells or other unnatural armour even as they feast upon the remains of their fellows. Missiles blast monsters off the chasm wall, knocking them from their purchase in showers of falling rock, while flamers cleanse the ledge. Urcus stands exhausted in his powerless plate as things of nightmare are blasted into oblivion, assuming ever more disgusting and riotous forms as they go.

The thunder of gunfire seems to last an eternity. But finally, as the last of the monstrous bodies tumbles back down into the gloom, silence reigns.

The Word Bearers are gone, and their unnatural darkness with them. For how long, Urcus does not like to guess.

He stares into the black depths that have claimed his captain – nay, his friend. The grief he feels is agonising, even in the overwhelming exhaustion and anguish that wracks both his body and soul. Power-armoured Ultramarines attend him, an Apothecary surveying his injuries.

He is greeted then by the outstretched gauntlet of an Honorarius of the 82nd Company, who takes his battered claw in a warrior's handshake.

'Obliged,' Urcus tells him. It is all that his tired mind can think to say. 'Thank you.'

'Your thanks go to Tetrarch Tauro Nicodemus, brother,' the

Ultramarine tells him. 'It is he who despatched this force for you and your captain, Steloc Aethon of the Nineteenth.'

Urcus glances back to the abyss. His hearts are leaden.

'My captain is dead.'

'I know, brother,' the Honorarius says quietly. 'Still, my Lord Nicodemus requests the honour of your reinforcement in the Arcology Magnesi system.'

'You came for us,' Urcus marvels. 'After we lost communications.'

'Aye, as it seems you did for us. We knew there must have been a connecting route between the two networks deeper through the sub-levels.'

'My captain thought the same thing,' Urcus says, leaving it at that. He straightens as best he can. 'I am Orestrian Urcus. Sergeant. Nineteenth Company.'

'Hylas Pelion,' the Honorarius tells him. 'Though my company call me Pelion the Lesser.'

'Then I should be honoured to do the same, brother.'

ABOUT THE AUTHOR

Rob Sanders is the author of 'The Serpent Beneath', a novella that appeared in the *New York Times* bestselling Horus Heresy anthology *The Primarchs*. His other Black Library credits include the Warhammer 40,000 titles *Adeptus Mechanicus: Skitarius* and *Tech-Priest*, *Legion of the Damned*, *Atlas Infernal* and *Redemption Corps* and the audio drama *The Path Forsaken*. He has also written the Warhammer Archaon duology, *Everchosen* and *Lord of Chaos* along with many Quick Reads for the Horus Heresy and Warhammer 40,000. He lives in the city of Lincoln, UK.

THE HORUS HERESY®

David Annandale

THE UNBURDENED

Betrayal at Calth

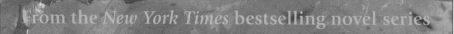

David Annandale

THE UNBURDENED

Betrayal at Calth

An extract from
The Unburdened
by David Annandale

'WE WILL HAVE the answers we seek before the day is done.'

Kurtha Sedd, Chaplain of the Fifth Assault Company, Chapter of the Third Hand, stood on the blasted plain that was the corpse and the grave of Monarchia. He repeated the words under his breath. No one else heard. He had removed his helm, and the sentence was swept away by the doleful wind. He repeated it again, with the doleful rhythm of a mourning bell. He was not the only one of his brothers whose spirit was held captive by that sentence. He heard others speak it, both nearby and over the vox. But the refrains he heard were at least as angry and determined as they were bewildered.

Was he the only one who regarded the promise of answers with sick dread?

The words were Lorgar's words, the last full sentence he had spoken to his sons before his vox-transmission to the fleet had been cut off and Guilliman had ordered the XVII Legion planetside.

Guilliman ordered. And we obeyed.

He forced that thought – and its attendant question *why?* – aside. There were other, much larger questions. Much worse ones. And the answers, he was sure, would be worse yet.

We will have the answers we seek before the day is done.

The words of the primarch were reality itself. It was not that Lorgar shaped reality with his speech. He was the son of a god, not a god himself. But in Lorgar's words, both written and voiced, Kurtha Sedd saw the total apprehension of the truth. Such was the depth of Lorgar's understanding. He had prophesied the coming of the Emperor to Colchis, and so the Emperor had come, as if summoned by the call of his son and the need of the world. Lorgar had brought the XVII Legion to the knowledge of the Emperor's godhood. Lorgar's words, truth, the real: there was no space between the concepts. This certainty was the bedrock of Kurtha Sedd's faith.

If Lorgar said answers would come, they would.

Kurtha Sedd did not want them to come. He could not imagine any answer that would not strike with the force of a cyclonic torpedo.

He took a deep breath. Unfiltered by his helm, the ruined air of Monarchia scraped into his throat and lungs. His mouth filled with the taste of betrayal. It was dust, it was ash, and it was the lingering heat of annihilation. His neuroglottis parsed the smell, telling what had burned. Stone and metal, wood and cloth. And yes, human flesh. Beyond what had been the outer walls of the perfect city was a displaced population of millions. The people wandered and mourned and tore their hair. They wept for their homes, they wept in incomprehension, and they wept for loved ones. There had been massacres here. People had resisted. People had chosen not to flee. They had died for their fidelity to the Emperor.

Kurtha Sedd tasted their martyrdom. He felt sick. *Blood demands blood.* Lorgar had said that too, when confronted by the scars on Khur, the evidence of the Ultramarines' crime. *Blood demands blood.* Perhaps. But that was a response, not an answer.

And the response had not come. What had happened to Monarchia defied all comprehension, and instead of attacking, the Word Bearers had obeyed the Ultramarines and descended to the site of destruction.

Kurtha Sedd turned around slowly, blinking away the grit that gathered on his eyelashes. Every direction was the same: the blackened ground, the great absence of the perfection that had stood here, and the gathering of his brothers. Thunderhawks stirred up billows of dust with their engines as they came in to land. As Word Bearers wandered over the fused, melted, pulverised remnants of Monarchia, the ash blew in swirls from their armour. Grey motes flew from grey masses, as if the armour itself were disintegrating.

We are eroding, Kurtha Sedd thought. A killing wind was blowing through the Legion. It was bad enough now. What would it be when the answers came?

'Chaplain?'

He blinked. Toc Derenoth stood before him. 'What is it, brother?' he asked the other legionary.

'We are gathering.' He pointed to Kurtha Sedd's left.

'Yes.' The Chaplain didn't look. He was gripped by a vision triggered by the close sight of the swirling ash and Toc Derenoth's power armour. It was a vision of erosion, yes, but of a particular kind. On the Word Bearer's right pauldron, the sunburst design and sinuous rune of the Third Hand were as bright and strong as ever. The parchments of devotion to the Emperor were turning grey in the air, darkening with filth, becoming illegible. The script on his armour, the indelible truths of the Imperium, appeared to be flaking off into the wind.

What am I seeing? Kurtha Sedd wondered.

The answer came between the beats of his hearts: truth crumbling. Truth that was eternal, that was the light for the entire galaxy. Breaking down, eaten by the wind, obscured by dust and flying away with ash.

Kurtha Sedd's instinct was to turn from the vision. He should shut his eyes to this blasphemy. But the discipline and duty of a Chaplain sustained him. His duty was to look deeper. His discipline gave him the tools to reach understanding.

The Imperial Truth vanishes. The Third Hand remains.

The core is freed of the distorting encrustation.

He grunted. The idea struck him to the core, a gladius sinking deep between his ribs. He hurled it away, but the wound remained. He could already feel it fester, as if he had been struck by something with the potency of actual insight.

Of truth.

Another deep breath. Another lungful of ruin. Then: 'Yes,' he said, again. He nodded to Toc Derenoth. He observed the current of movement, the Legion forming up and advancing to a centre that no longer existed. He began to march.

Around him, the Fifth Assault Company assumed formation and purpose.

Legionary Kaeloq approached from his left. Kurtha Sedd had spoken with him and Toc Derenoth often over the years. Both warriors had deep, laudable hungers for understanding, and a talent for exegesis. But where Toc Derenoth's study of the Word and the Truth led him from one question to another, Kaeloq's quest was for answers. He was devoted to the hierarchy of spiritual leadership in descent from the Emperor to the primarch, from the primarch to the Chaplains.

'Are we at war, Chaplain?' Kaeloq asked.

'What do you think, brother?' Kurtha Sedd made it a practice to redirect Kaeloq's questions back at him. The easily gained answer, even though true, would lack the proper strength of revelation. But this time, there was nothing rhetorical or instructive about his response. His question was genuine.

'It's an attack, but it makes no tactical sense,' Kaeloq said, struggling as they all were with the inexplicable. 'And we were not fired upon when we arrived.'

'And why would we be at war with a brother Legion?' said Toc Derenoth.

The Chaplain didn't answer. The vox crackled with silence. Even though Toc Derenoth had phrased his question as a denial, rejecting the idea even as he gave it form, just saying the words was to give voice to something monstrous.

Legion against Legion. Such unimaginable fratricide would crack the materium in half. There was no other way reality could respond to that impossibility.

And yet Monarchia was ash.

And the air was filled with the taste of a truth that could not be spoken.

'*Surely some revelation is at hand,*' Kurtha Sedd muttered.

'What do you mean, Chaplain?' Toc Derenoth asked.

Kurtha Sedd shook his head. 'Nothing. Something. I don't know, brother. I was quoting an ancient remembrancer of Terra. Yaitz. The fragments of his work that have come down to us have been interpreted as prophesying the coming of the Emperor.'

Surely some revelation is at hand.

We will have the answers we seek.

His life as Chaplain had been devoted to the Truth, and to its discovery, its praise, and its propagation. And now, how he dreaded its coming. He would hold it back if he could. And yet, he refused to don his helm. He refused to filter the murdered air of Monarchia. He was taking truth on board with every breath, and with every breath something fractured a bit more, something more than vital, something that should never break.

He walked through the cinders. His steps kicked up small clouds of particulate. A weight pressed down on his shoulders, growing more massive as the time for answers drew near.

The Word Bearers assembled for their answers. Rank upon rank of warriors in grey. As Toc Derenoth and Kaeloq fell back, rejoining their squad, Kurtha Sedd advanced with the other Chaplains and the captains. He opened a vox-channel to the full company. 'The Word is our burden,' he said. 'Nothing can surpass its holy weight. Whatever this day brings, brothers of the Seventeenth Legion, know that we will shoulder it.'

Clicks and mutters of assent answered him. Then he broke the connection. He didn't trust himself to speak without doubt working its way into his voice.

He didn't even trust the sound of his breathing.

WHEN, AFTER THE wounds of the day had scabbed over sufficiently for them to be discussed at all, Kurtha Sedd found, as he had suspected, that he was one of the first to feel the greater betrayals. Before the Rebuke, before the primarch confronted his father, even before Guilliman and the Sigillite appeared, Kurtha Sedd was staggered by the sight of the Ultramarines banners. A hundred warriors in blue descended the ramps of their Thunderhawks, and a white horse on an azure field shone with pride through the haze.

The 19th Company.

Aethon, Kurtha Sedd thought. He managed to remain upright.

He realised that, until this moment, he had nurtured an unconscious hope: that Aethon did not know about, or at the very least did not condone, the crime perpetrated on Khur. The idea of the Ultramarines turning on another Legion was mad, but the madness did not bear the face of a friend. He needed to hang on to something. There must be stability somewhere. The entire universe could not have fallen to madness. But there was Aethon at the head of his company. He not only knew, he had participated in the destruction.

The ground beneath Kurtha Sedd's feet was thin as ice, changeable as sand.

Why? Kurtha Sedd wanted to reach across the space between the Word Bearers and Ultramarines, across the emptiness that had once been the Inaga Sector, and shake the warrior at whose side he had fought so many campaigns. *Why?* he wanted to cry to his friend. The legionary whose life he had saved on Melior-Tertia, the brother with whom he had celebrated victories, with whom he had debated the finer points of the Imperial Truth.

His trust in Aethon was adamantine. Every joint campaign between the Word Bearers and the Ultramarines had cemented the bond forged during the vanquishing of the orks.

Trust. Loyalty. Brotherhood. The belief in these concepts and the need for their reality were chains, wrapped so tight around his chest and throat that he could not breathe. They trapped him. They pushed down on his soul, crushing instead of freeing.

Aethon was here. Aethon knew. There was the first answer. If the first was so terrible, how much worse would the others be?

He tried to brace himself.

The effort was futile. The hammer blows began.

How much worse?

They would be enough to force him to his knees.

The answers came, one after another. Their impact was cumulative. The ends of Kurtha Sedd's fingers buzzed. A sensation both numbing and agonising crawled up his limbs as all that was real crumbled, and the impossible rioted. His vision was blasted by the sight of everything he knew to be, ground into the ashes of Monarchia.

He saw Lorgar and Guilliman, the demi-god brothers, at odds. He saw Lorgar strike Malcador the Sigillite and, though the mortal fell like a bundle of brittle sticks, it was Lorgar who seemed impotent, his violence the futile striking-out of the vanquished. Impossible, of course.

And then the worst thing of all. Kurtha Sedd beheld the divine. He beheld the God-Emperor. His eyes burned. He thought he would go blind, yet he could no more avert his gaze than take to the air. He was forced to watch, even as his consciousness fragmented.

He saw his primarch plead with the greatest Father.

He saw a god reject worship and turn in anger on his most faithful children.

And worst of all, he heard the Emperor speak to him. To every Word Bearer. There were many words, but it was the first that was the most important. The most fatal. The one that brought the weight of all existence down on Kurtha Sedd's shoulders, and shattered the foundation of his strength.

So much from a single word.

+Kneel.+

IN THE DAYS that followed, Kurtha Sedd would know all the events of the Rebuke with perfect clarity. He would know every detail of the humiliation, and every syllable uttered. But he would know these things as if they had been reported to him. Their coherence was at a distance. His own experience of them was a raw, burning, slashing, bleeding maelstrom of injury and howling memory. In his lived experience, in the visceral, in the roar of his soul, there was no coherence.

Nor should there be. The Emperor forced the Word Bearers to their knees. What logic could exist after that?

The hours after the Rebuke were lost to him. They existed as fragments. There were impressions of ordered movement – his battle-brothers marching again, humiliation and lost purpose in their gait. There were the engine gales of one

Thunderhawk after another taking off. No memory was complete. They were a blur of grey. Armour and ash and dust and faith all one, all vanishing. Only one fragment was vivid. It was of Sor Gharax.

Kurtha Sedd heard the Contemptor Dreadnought raging. That was not new. Sor Gharax had been descending into darker and darker fugues of anger and bitterness since his entombment in the war-shell. His injuries during the campaign to bring Seventeen-Seventeen into compliance had been more than physical. Now, though, his ranting was more venomous than ever. It was barely coherent. Kurtha Sedd made out only a few of the phrases. One cycle ago, he would have considered what he heard blasphemous. They were repetitions of the Emperor's own words, but the hate in the echo was monstrous. The Word Bearers close to Sor Gharax turned their heads from him, as if to deny the echoing howls of the venerable warrior.

Of course Sor Gharax howled. Existence itself should have been destroyed by the Emperor's act. But it was not. There was still earth beneath Kurtha Sedd's boots when he became aware of his surroundings again.

It was night. He was no longer in the grave of Monarchia. The stench of the destruction was still in his nostrils, and the ash still turned the air grey, but the land he walked was not cinder and glass. In the distance, to his left, he heard the clamour and lamentation from one of the vast refugee camps that had sprung up outside the city's former boundaries. Millions upon millions of civilians had been displaced. The people had nowhere to go. Monarchia and fifteen other great cities were gone. None of Khur's remaining centres had the means to absorb influxes many times larger than their current populations. And the nearest city of any size was hundreds of kilometres from Monarchia.

'Is this reason?' Kurtha Sedd rasped, and for the first time in his life, he questioned the Emperor. 'Is this truth? Is this justice? We brought this population into compliance for you. We taught them to worship you. They were guilty of nothing except absolute fidelity to your name. And so they must be punished in order to make an example of *us*. Are their lives meaningless, then? Their catastrophe unimportant except as a means to an end? You needed a Legion to kneel in dust, but first you needed the dust.'

'Chaplain Kurtha Sedd, to whom are you speaking?' The voice on the vox came from a huge distance. Too far to be of any importance. But it kept calling his name, an insistent insect. *'Chaplain, respond.'* The voice belonged to Tergothar, the captain of the Fifth Assault Company.

Kurtha Sedd hadn't realised he had left his vox open. His words would have been transmitted to the entire company.

Good. He surprised himself with the thought.

He clicked in answer to Tergothar, but said nothing.

'Brother-Chaplain, we are leaving Khur. The order has been given for immediate embarkation. We must–'

Kurtha Sedd broke the connection and silenced the vox. He looked over, back in the direction of Monarchia. Thunder-hawks rose on trails of fire through the smoke. They clawed their way towards the clouds. The Word Bearers were departing the scene of their humiliation.

He could not. Not yet. The wound was too deep and too fresh.

He marched on. He felt as if he were stumbling, but his boots hit the ground with each step as if they would crush the bedrock itself. The wind picked up. Dust ticked against his armour. It stung his flesh. It caked his nostrils, numbing his sense of smell. The cries of the Khur cocooned him. He retreated into his pain. The shriek of the wind was the sound of meaninglessness. He began to run. He did not know whether he was retreating from the pyre of faith or charging towards the void of hope.

There was a weight in his right hand. It dragged at him. He lifted the object. He held it before him as he ran. It was his crozius arcanum. The weapon was his staff of office. It was the symbol of his purpose. But his god had declared his purpose a lie. He held a symbol with no referent. His occulobe magnified the weak light of Khur's moon shining through the cloud cover, and before his eyes the ornamentations of the metal appeared to writhe. They were seeking a new configuration, a new purpose.

He ran. Through dust and night, through nothing and towards nothing, holding a thing of metal and power, a weapon as dead and as hungry, as searching and as agonised as he was. He saw nothing except the crozius. He shut out the world. The wind and the dust were the static of reality, idiot sensation and noise, symptoms of a universal disease.

There was no time in the void through which he moved. He was suspended in a limbo of spiritual laceration. He would have run through the night, but a noise reached his consciousness. It drew him back to the world. He turned with a snarl in the direction of the sound. He froze when he recognised it: voices raised in prayer.

He was standing near the intersection of eight highways. Dust blew in serpentine twists over the rockcrete. The roads met in a traffic circle around a low elevation of granite. Eight staircases rose up to a house of worship that seemed to grow out of the rock itself. Kurtha Sedd stared, at first unable to understand where the chapel had come from. It was no cathedral, but it was large enough, its cluster of spires and gold-rimmed vaulted doorways imposing in isolation. There were no other buildings in the vicinity. There was no settlement within kilometres of his position. Then he remembered that this was precisely the point: he was looking at a wayfarers' chapel. They dotted Khur, having sprung up in locations far from the major centres, but on the principal routes between them. Here the people could stop in their travels, rest and meditate, and express their love for the God-Emperor. The god who rejected their love.

Kurtha Sedd walked towards the chapel. There were numerous vehicles pulled off on the verges. Most were on the road from Monarchia. More refugees, fleeing the terror of the Ultramarines. They had not heard the news of the day. They still lived in a galaxy where the worship of the Emperor was the most natural and needful thing.

He donned his helm. He looked at the world with the eyes of a hunter. This was what he was, after all.

Wage war as you were created to do. The Emperor's words. The Emperor's command. Do not worship. Spread nothing but conquest.

Kurtha Sedd pushed the doors open. He walked into a scene of untroubled faith. The pews were full. There were more than a thousand people present. They were dirty from travelling. The aisles were clogged with bundles of hastily assembled possessions. Many of the worshippers were weeping, but their voices were strong in their pleas for help and their praise of the god. Their homes had been destroyed, but they had hope. They had their belief. It was adamantine. It would support them.

The doors shut behind Kurtha Sedd with a dull clang. He stood in the chapel, the sole being deprived of succour. He was the Chaplain of an apostate god.

The people turned to look at him. A collective sigh of joy rose to the chapel vaults. Then came a babble of voices, and from it emerged variations of the same words: *angel… true angel… grey angel…*

The nearest celebrants, still on their knees, reached out to touch his cloak. They cried out their thanks. *Saved,* they said, again and again.

Kurtha Sedd slowly turned his head back and forth, taking in every detail of the scene, every soul present, hearing the joy in the voices, seeing the faith in the eyes. Hearing the lie. Seeing the lie.

The wounds of the Rebuke stabbed deeper and deeper. The universe was devoid of anything except grief and rage and betrayal. He had devoted his life to the truth, and now the font of truth had denied itself. In this moment, when he needed to feel the strength of truth more than at any other time in his existence, he did not know if there was any truth at all beyond the lack of all meaning.

Rage in his bones. Hate in his limbs. His fist tightened on the haft of the crozius. The symbol in search of meaning. The weapon in search of blood.

'You believe the Emperor has heard your prayers,' he said. His helm speakers amplified his voice. The growl bounced off the walls. It filled the space with the iron of his pain. 'You are correct. He has heard them. *And he has come in anger. There will be no prayer. Obey him and turn from him!'*

There was a confused silence. He could see the ripple of bafflement move over the crowd. Then the silence turned into shouts, and they were still confused, but there was also refusal. It emerged from the roar of questions and shouts, clear and strong and fanatical. What he had said was not true. What he had said was nonsensical. What he had said could not be accepted.

The people were right. But the Emperor had said otherwise. And so what was right was wrong.

Grief and betrayal and rage. Growing and festering with the beats of his hearts, merging into a single passion, one with no name and no expression except violence. A haze descended over his sight. He saw black and red and truth and lies and there was no distinguishing between them.

'*You will not worship!*' he roared. *Our god commands it*, he thought.

But the people shouted louder and louder, calling on the Emperor and his angels. Their praise grew more desperate. With panicked fidelity, the handful of worshippers clutching at his cloak held it now as if to hold him in their world. Their desperation overwhelmed the awe that would have held them back from daring to touch his being.

'*Silence!*' he shouted, and his agony was such that it should have torn the chapel asunder. Why did the air not bleed? Why did the stars not bleed?

And there was no silence. Only an ever-greater cacophony of prayer and plea and song.

And the haze. Darker. Deeper. Flashing with the nova intensity of despair.

Kurtha Sedd tilted his head back. '*This is your will!*' he said in defiance and obedience to the god whose back had turned. *'This is your command!'* he said in hate and love, faith and disbelief. He raised the crozius. It was suddenly filled with a purpose he could not name. *'Release me!'* he said, but though he looked down, he was not speaking to the people gathered at his feet. Nor did he give them time to obey. He swung the crozius. With a single sweep of his arm, he smashed four heads to spray and flying bone. The bodies fell away from him. The hands let go of his cloak. Though the tugging had been weak, as he smashed the mortal burdens he felt a monstrous liberation.

He swung the crozius again. Blood splashed over his helm. His eyes saw red through red. The crack of bone and the tearing of muscle was the smashing of fetters. The shouts became screams. They were not loud enough. He could barely hear them through the roaring of his voice, the roaring in his head, and the roaring of the universe. So he struck again, and again, faster, striding through the aisles, pulling out his plasma pistol as the crowd surged for the exits, summoning more fear, more death, more shrieks, and still the screams were not loud enough. With his right hand, he battered the worshippers to shapeless pulp. With his left, he brought fire from the heart of a sun to each doorway.

With each blow, with each pull of the trigger, something broke inside. A part of him was wailing in horror, but he drowned that part in blood. Every death was another drop into the abyss, and the plunge was exhilarating. There was no difference between self-loathing and freedom. He was destroying everything he had been, but everything he had stood for had already been taken from him.

The fall accelerated. He killed faster and faster, and he roared without words, shouting nothing at nothing, voiding his soul. With fire and iron he transformed the outer world into the mirror of his slaughtered faith. He destroyed order. He destroyed sense. He destroyed truth.

Red of blood. Red of flame. Red of screams.

Red of ending.

He waded through bodies. Then there were so many dead that he was climbing over the mounds of his butchery. He needed more screams. He needed more blood as he fulfilled the Emperor's decree to its most obscene limit. He could not kill fast enough. He fired the plasma pistol without pause, pushing it past its critical point.

The weapon overheated. The venting of the cooling ducts could not keep up with the rate of fire. The gun preserved its integrity with an emergency release. A cloud of super-heated gas burst from the barrel. It enveloped Kurtha Sedd. It flashed through the entire space of the chapel, an expanding bubble of wrath itself. The readouts of his auto-senses screamed red, and were lost in the crimson sea of his frenzy. The outer layers of his armour flash-boiled. The flesh of the congregation vaporised. The heat reached through his armour, through the grille of his rebreather. His lungs took in the wrath, and they withered. He staggered, and his arms dropped to his side.

The incinerating gas cloud dissipated, leaving scorched walls and wet bones contorted in the instant of excruciating death. The red haze faded. He smelled blood and burned bodies. His auto-senses still flashed damage alerts. He blinked them off. He stood in the centre of the chapel, surrounded by his works, listening to the sound of his breathing, to his pulse, and to the thickening silence.

What have you done?

The hundreds of worshippers were mounds of blackened meat and broken shapes.

What have you done?

As rationality returned, a vertigo of disassociation took him. Who had committed this crime? He must have witnessed it from a distance, but he could not be responsible. The denial collapsed almost as soon as it took form. In its wake came a dread from the depths of his soul.

He knows what you have done.

There was a memory that had been the source of his greatest pride and the spur to his calling as Chaplain. It was a memory that had shaped him and his actions. It was the memory of Lorgar's words to him, at the dawn of his existence as a Space Marine: 'The Emperor is watching you.'

The Emperor was a god, and so the words were a literal truth. He had crusaded under that omniscient gaze. He had devoted his life to proving himself worthy of its favour.

He knows what you have done.

The Emperor had denied his divinity, but he had done so with divine power. He had judged the Word Bearers. He had made them kneel. A hundred thousand of them. With a single thought.

He knows what you have done.

Judgement must surely come.

Kurtha Sedd stood, and he waited. The silence grew heavy. It pressed on him as if he were at the bottom of an ocean. The ache in his chest was deep, hollow, filled with the swirl of dust.

An hour or an age passed. He heard a door open at his back. He did not turn. He heard the tread of ceramite boots on the stone floor. They stopped just inside the entrance.

Judgement has come.

Instead, a familiar voice said, 'Chaplain, what has happened?'

Now he turned around. Toc Derenoth stood as motionless as he himself had been moments before. Behind the legionary came Kaeloq, then Captain Tergothar. Each appeared to take root as he encountered the abattoir.

Tergothar acted first. 'Wait outside,' he commanded unseen battle-brothers. Then he closed the door. 'Chaplain?' he said.

Kurtha Sedd made no answer. *Where is judgement?* he wondered.

'Can you hear me?' said Tergothar.

Kurtha Sedd could. He turned his vox back on, but he was listening to the greater silence beyond. He was listening to an emptiness that could not be.

'Take him outside,' said the captain.

Toc Derenoth and Kaeloq walked to Kurtha Sedd's position in the transept. Bodies crunched beneath their steps. Some broke into powder. The two Word Bearers moved to either side of him. Toc Derenoth placed his hand on Kurtha Sedd's right shoulder. 'Come with us, Chaplain,' he said.

Kurtha Sedd let himself be guided forwards. He started walking. His legs moved. His feet trod the floor of the chapel. He saw his actions but did not feel them. He was numb. The dread of judgement was giving way to the worse experience of absence.

'Where is he?' Kurtha Sedd whispered.

'Who?' Kaeloq asked.

'Exactly.' A breath wheezed from Kurtha Sedd's lungs. It was the bitter laugh of absolute despair. 'Exactly so. Who is he?'

Is he a god? Where is his judgement? Is he right to deny his divinity? Is Lorgar wrong? Did Lorgar lie?

The numbing limbo was inviting. If he submerged himself in it, perhaps the questions would not pursue him. The very articulation of those questions was a torture and an obscenity. Their answers could only be worse. The contradictions were beyond resolving. The truth, whatever form it took, could not be borne.

He did not succumb. The questions were too strong, and he was no coward. He had always fought for the truth, or at least what he had believed it to be. When at last it revealed itself to him, he would not turn from it. But for now, there were only the questions, and the incomprehension, and the horror, and the blood on his hands.

So much blood. Even though the vitae had been burned away along with the layers of his armour, he thought he could still see it. Instead of grey, he was crimson. Word and act and blood and being were all one now.

He exited the chapel. Toc Derenoth and Kaeloq walked with him down the steps to the dust-blown roads. Brothers from the Fifth waited outside the doors, lined the stairs, and gathered on the rockcrete. Four Thunderhawks rested on the roads. Tergothar had brought a large force in search of him. Kurtha Sedd wondered why. The captain could hardly have thought he had been captured. They were not at war, after all. The humiliation had been delivered, and the Ultramarines had departed. They were mere messengers, blindly following orders, and their work was done.

Perhaps Tergothar had expected something extreme on Kurtha Sedd's part. He had a reputation for recklessness on the battlefield. He took the mad risks, sustained by the confidence of his faith.

And now? he thought. *What have you done now?*

He had no answer. There were no words. There was no Word. It had been broken by the Emperor.

There was a scratching at his ear. It cut through the limbo, irritating, drawing his attention. It was Tergothar's voice on the vox. *'Burn everything,'* Tergothar said. *'Bring the chapel down. Leave no trace.'*

Toc Derenoth and Kaeloq guided Kurtha Sedd towards a Thunderhawk. He stopped short of the loading ramp. He turned to watch Tergothar's orders carried out. Word Bearers entered the chapel. After a few moments, flames erupted from the doorways and broken windows. As the legionaries exited, the other three gunships took off. They flew in a circle formation over the chapel. Their cannons poured shells into the structure. The foundations erupted. The walls collapsed in on each other. Fragments of spire cartwheeled skywards, a last gesture of prayer, then fell down into the holocaust. Fire, smoke and dust rose higher and spread outwards. They consumed. They obscured.

They erased.

Kurtha Sedd saw all trace of his crime expunged. The cannon barrage continued, battering even the rocky elevation to powder. Soon there would be nothing but a crater. The knowledge of what had happened would be buried deep within the Legion.

Kurtha Sedd had no doubt the massacre would be concealed. The knowledge filled him with wracking grief. The Emperor did not watch him. Lorgar had lied. The universe was empty of anything except betrayal. There was no room for faith.

But guilt, the corpse of faith, would not lie still. It thrashed back and forth in his chest. *Where is the judgement?* it asked, over and over, obsessed, unable to accept *nowhere* as an answer.

Where is the judgement? Where is the judgement?

He had sinned. He must answer. He could not shed the burden of this truth.

Where is the judgement?

It will come.

When?

When?

When?